BLOOD IS THICKER . . .

"You're gonna pay now," Pete said as he gathered his legs under him.

Behind him Hank was doing the same thing.

As Pete reached his feet a split second before his brother, Clint knew he was going to go for his gun, and he got there first. He snatched the man's gun from his holster before Pete knew it, stunning the man.

"How'd you do that?" Pete demanded.

"Never mind," Clint said. He trained Pete's gun on both men. "You, put your gun on the bar."

Hank stared into the barrel of his brother's gun, and then complied.

"Now get out, both of you."

DON'T MISS THESE
ALL-ACTION WESTERN SERIES
FROM THE BERKLEY PUBLISHING GROUP

THE GUNSMITH by J. R. Roberts
  Clint Adams was a legend among lawmen, outlaws, and ladies. They called him . . . the Gunsmith.

LONGARM by Tabor Evans
  The popular long-running series about U.S. Deputy Marshal Long—his life, his loves, his fight for justice.

SLOCUM by Jake Logan
  Today's longest-running action Western. John Slocum rides a deadly trail of hot blood and cold steel.

BUSHWHACKERS by B. J. Lanagan
  An all-new series by the creators of Longarm! The rousing adventures of the most brutal gang of cutthroats ever assembled—Quantrill's Raiders.

THE GUNSMITH

193

TEXAS WIND

J. R. ROBERTS

J
JOVE BOOKS, NEW YORK

TEXAS WIND

A Jove Book / published by arrangement with
the author

PRINTING HISTORY
Jove edition / February 1998

The Putnam Berkley World Wide Web site address is
http://www.berkley.com

ISBN: 0-515-12231-9

A JOVE BOOK®
Jove Books are published by The Berkley Publishing Group, a member
of Penguin Putnam Inc.,
200 Madison Avenue, New York, New York 10016.
JOVE and the "J" design are trademarks
belonging to Jove Publications, Inc.

PRINTED IN THE UNITED STATES OF AMERICA

10 9 8 7 6 5 4 3 2 1

ONE

"They're going to force your hand," the sheriff said to Clint Adams.

Clint looked at him over the rim of his beer mug, then put the mug down on the table.

"Why don't you stop them?"

"They haven't broken the law."

"So you'll just stand by and watch?"

The man shrugged. Clint had been in the town of Hampton, Missouri, for three days, and each day he had come to like Sheriff Tank Willard less and less—but never less than today.

"You don't think much of me as a lawman, do you, Adams?" Willard asked.

"No, I don't . . . Sheriff."

"Well, then," Willard said, standing up, "maybe that explains why I'm gonna enjoy standing by and watching them kill you."

Clint looked up at the man and decided to make him squirm.

"When this is over, Sheriff," he said, "I'll come looking for you."

The sheriff looked uncomfortable for a moment before catching himself and hiding it.

1

"If you get by the Jensens," he said, "but I don't think I have to worry about that. There's three of them and one of you."

"Just remember what I said," Clint told him. He really didn't expect to waste his time with the fool, but it was good to see the weasel cringe.

"Yeah . . ." the sheriff said, and slunk out of the saloon.

Outside Linc Jensen saw the sheriff coming across the street.

"Get 'im," Linc said to his brothers, Pete and Hank.

Pete drew his gun.

"No," Linc said, "I don't mean shoot 'im, I mean bring him here so I can talk to him . . . you dummy."

"Maw wouldn't like you callin' me no dummy," Pete said, putting his gun away.

"Maw's dead, you dummy," Linc said. "Go on, get him and bring him here."

"Come on," Hank said, grabbing Pete's arm.

Linc watched his two brothers intercept the sheriff, grab his arms, and bring him over. Both Pete and Hank were over six feet, and standing between them the sheriff looked like a short man, even though he was about five ten.

"Hey, Linc . . ." the sheriff said nervously.

"What'd he say, Tank?"

"Nothin' much, Linc."

"Is he comin' out?"

"Eventually, I guess."

"And he didn't say nothin'?"

"Well . . ."

"What'd he say?"

"He said he was gonna come for me when he was finished with you."

Linc looked across the street at the saloon.

"Arrogant son of a bitch!"

"Yeah . . ." Willard said. "Uh, Linc, can I go back to my office now?"

Linc waved his hand in reply and said, "Go on, stay outta my way."

"I can do that," Willard said, and hurried away to his office.

"What are we gonna do, Linc?" Hank asked his older brother.

"We're gonna do what I said we're gonna do," Linc said. "We're gonna wait out here for as long as it takes, and we're gonna kill us a Gunsmith."

"He's supposed to be fast, Linc," Pete said, "real fast."

Linc gave his brother a hard look.

"And I ain't?"

"You're fast, Linc," Hank said, shaking his head at his brother Pete.

"Real fast," Pete said.

"I could take him alone if I wanted to," Lincoln Jensen said.

"Sure you could, Linc," Pete said.

"I just don't want to deprive you boys of gettin' some of the credit."

"Right, Linc," Hank said.

"So we'll just wait for him to come out," Linc continued, "no matter how long it takes."

"Right, Linc," Pete said.

"No matter how long," Hank said.

"It's too bad Maw ain't here to see it," Hank said. "She'd be proud of us."

"Real proud," Pete agreed. When his older brother didn't reply he asked, "Wouldn't she, Linc?"

"Sure," Linc Jensen said, "sure, boys, she'd be real proud of her sons. Now shut up and keep your eyes on the front of the saloon."

TWO

Grace Whitney looked out over the batwing doors, then turned and started walking to the table Clint was sitting at. The Bull & Bear Saloon was empty except for her; Clint; Dan, the bartender; and Clive Lovejoy, the Englishman who owned the place.

"I say," Clive said to Clint, "you're not doing a lot for my business, you know."

Clive was sitting across the room at his own table, playing solitaire.

"Tell it to the Jensen boys," Clint said. He looked at Grace. "Are they still out there?"

"Yep," she said, "they haven't moved."

She was blond, solidly built, a handsome woman rather than pretty. She and Clint had hit it off the first day he was in town and had spent the last three nights together.

She walked to his table, put her hands on her hips, and stared down at him.

"You gonna get yourself killed?"

He smiled at her.

"Not if I can help it."

"Are you goin' out there?"

"Eventually."

"Those boys have been stalking you for three days,"

she said, "and you been puttin' them off. Why today?"

"It's got to end sometime, Grace."

"And it's going to end with you dead."

"Again," he said, "not if I can help it."

"I don't know about Hank and Pete," she said, "but I've seen Linc shoot, and he's good."

"That's what I heard, too."

"Are you as good as they say you are?"

"Well, I don't know, Grace," he said, leaning back in his chair, "how good do they say I am?"

"Some say real good," she said. "Some say the best."

"Well," he said, "I guess the truth lies somewhere in the middle, then."

She sat down at the table with him.

"Is there any way I can convince you to go out the back door?"

He sat forward again, tried to look at her face and not her impressive cleavage.

"What would be the point?" Clive asked before Clint could reply.

She turned her head and looked at him.

"What do you mean?"

"They would simply track him down again," Clive said. "Why not get it over with today?"

"You just want him to go out there because you know when it's all over everybody's going to be back in here looking for a drink. There's nothing like a killing to make everybody thirsty—everybody who's alive, that is."

"Leave him alone, Grace," Clint said. "He's got a right to want his business back."

"Not at the expense of your life."

Clint reached across the table and covered her hands with one of his.

"You stay inside."

She snatched her hands away.

"You bet I'll stay inside," she snapped. "I don't want to see you get killed. There's three of them out there,

Clint, and at least one of them can shoot. One of the others might even hit you by accident.''

"You're not showing a lot of confidence in me, Grace," Clint said.

"It doesn't matter how good you are, Clint," she said, "anything can happen."

"You're right about that," Clint said.

"You know that?"

"Sure I do," he said. "I'm not stupid, Grace."

"I know you're not."

"Anything can happen anytime, and anywhere," he said. "I could walk out that door right now and get run over by a buckboard."

"Or shot," she said.

"Or shot," he agreed. "And I'll tell you the truth. I'd rather get shot."

"Both are a wasteful way to die," Clive said.

"Well," Grace said, "that's the first intelligent thing you've said all day."

Clive raised his eyes from the cards on the table, pointed his hawk nose at Grace and regarded her gravely.

"How about 'you're fired'?"

"Again?" she asked, and turned away. Clive looked down at his cards again.

The bartender came over to the table.

"Another beer, Mr. Adams?"

"And look at you," Grace said to him.

"What?"

"You're a grown man in your thirties and you fawn all over Clint like you were a twelve-year-old impressed by a gunman's reputation."

"What are you picking on Dan for?" Clint asked. He looked at the bartender. "No thanks, Dan, no more for me—and don't let her bother you."

"Aw, she don't bother me," he said, even though he walked away with a wounded look on his face.

"Stop snapping at people," Clint said.

"I'm mad."

"At me," Clint said, "not at them. Okay, I guess it's time."

"Why?" she asked, looking alarmed. "Why now?"

"Maybe you'll be in a better mood when it's all over," he said, standing up.

"Oh, fine," she said, "now I can really feel guilty when you go out there and get shot."

Clint cupped her chin in his hand, leaned over, and kissed her warm, generous mouth.

"Just wait for me right here, Grace," he said.

"Damn you," she said, her eyes shining with tears, "if you get killed I'll never speak to you again."

"And I'll deserve it," he said.

THREE

Clint walked to the front doors of the saloon and looked outside. The street was empty, because people knew what was coming. He had no doubt that many of the citizens of Hampton were at their windows.

Across the street he saw the three Jensen brothers. When he had first arrived in town he'd had a problem with two of them, the two younger ones, Hank and Pete. It seemed Pete thought Clint was looking at him in the saloon and took offense. Clint tried to explain that he wasn't looking at him, but Pete took offense at that, too. Seemed he thought Clint was calling him a liar . . .

"I never said you were a liar," Clint said. "In fact, I didn't say anything, except that I wasn't looking at you."

"And that's callin' me a liar!" Pete shouted.

They were standing at the bar, Clint and the two Jensen boys, and a bunch of other men, and suddenly the others faded away, giving Clint and the brothers all the room they might need.

"Look," Clint said, "I'm not looking for trouble—"

"Well, you found it," Hank said, "when you called my brother a liar."

Clint wondered if it was possible for two brothers to be as dumb as one another.

"Look," he said, "you boys have been here longer than I have, and you've had more to drink. Why don't you both just go home and sleep it off."

"Now we're drunks," Pete said to Hank.

"I ain't no drunk," Hank said.

Pete was standing the closest to Clint, and now he moved even closer.

"You better take that back, mister," he said, and Clint realized he was dealing with at least one man—possibly two—who had the mind of a child.

"Get out of my face," Clint said, and with that he put his hand in Pete's face and shoved—hard.

Pete staggered back into his brother, who tried to catch him but staggered himself under his brother's weight, and abruptly both brothers were on their asses on the floor. The place exploded in laughter, or the incident might have ended right there.

Both brothers looked around at the laughing throng, and their faces flushed angrily, and with embarrassment.

As they started to get up Clint said, "Stay down."

"You're gonna pay now," Pete said as he gathered his legs under him.

Behind him Hank was doing the same thing.

As Pete reached his feet a split second before his brother, Clint knew he was going to go for his gun, and he got there first. He snatched the man's gun from his holster before Pete knew it, stunning the man.

"How'd you do that?" Pete demanded.

"Never mind," Clint said. He trained Pete's gun on both men. "You, put your gun on the bar."

Hank stared into the barrel of his brother's gun, and then complied.

"Now get out, both of you."

"Oh, not without our guns," Hank said.

"Mister," Pete said, "our brother will kill us if we go home without our guns."

"Then you'll have to explain that you lost them by being a couple of idiots. Now get out!"

Both men hesitated.

"You can pick up your guns tomorrow at the sheriff's office. Now get!"

This time they both moved, the laughter of the crowd echoing in their ears as they went out the front doors.

Clint put Pete's gun on the bar next to Hank's.

"Mister," the bartender—to whom Clint had not yet been introduced—said, "do you know who those boys were?"

"No, I don't," Clint said, picking up his beer. "Should I?"

"If you're gonna stay in this town for any amount of time you should. Them were the Jensen boys."

"So?"

"Their brother is Linc Jensen."

"The one who's going to kill them when they come home without their guns?"

"That's him."

"I never heard of him."

"Well," Dan said, "you will. . . ."

Clint looked across at the brothers now, picking Linc out easily. He was the smallest of the three, but the oldest and—supposedly—the smartest. He was also the one most of the people in town were afraid of, including the sheriff.

The three men had been following him around ever since he'd embarrassed two of them, only he was given to understand that embarrassing them meant he'd embarrassed the whole family.

"There's nothing I can do to help you," the sheriff had told him. "The Jensen boys usually get what they want, and it's usually because of Linc."

Clint didn't know how good Linc Jensen was with a gun, but he guessed this was as good a time as any to find out. He was tired of looking over his shoulder.

He stepped outside.

FOUR

"Here he comes, Linc," Hank said.

"I see him," Linc said, annoyed. Since the death of their mother a couple of years earlier he'd been taking care of both these boys, but he was starting to get tired of it. With the name he'd make for himself by killing Clint Adams he'd be able to get away from this town, and them.

"What do we do, Linc?" Pete asked. The quaver in his voice betrayed his nervousness.

"Just follow my lead, boys," Linc said. "I'll do most of the work, but you boys have got to back me up. Understand?"

"Sure, Linc," Hank said.

Pete didn't answer.

"Pete?"

"Huh? Oh, sure, Linc. Whatever you say."

"Then let's do it," Linc said, and stepped down into the street, followed by his two brothers.

Sheriff Tank Willard watched from his office window as Clint Adams and the three Jensen boys all stepped into the street and started toward each other. He didn't know if Adams could kill all three, but he hoped he'd at least

13

take care of Linc. With him out of the way, life would be much easier in Hampton.

Clint watched as the three brothers stepped into the street. The one in the middle was the one he didn't know, the older one, Linc. He was dressed in worn clothes like his brothers, but the gun and gun belt he had on were better quality than theirs. This was a man who took care of his weapon.

His brothers seemed nervous, especially the younger one. He was the one who had started the progression to this point, and he seemed the most nervous. He was brave enough in the saloon, with one brother behind him and a belly full of liquor. Now, though, backed by both brothers, he seemed scared. Clint didn't think he needed to concern himself with Pete. Not immediately, anyway. He doubted the man could hit him even if he managed to get the gun out of his holster.

The second brother, Hank, seemed a bit nervous, but not nearly to the extent his younger brother was.

It was clear that Linc was the main danger. No matter what happened, Clint's first shot was going to have to be for him.

"That's far enough," Linc called out. He wanted enough distance so that he and his brothers would have enough room, but Clint kept coming. If he got close to them they'd feel cramped, and it might interfere with their accuracy.

"I said far enough!" Linc shouted.

"I'll decide when it's far enough," Clint said. "I want to see your faces, your eyes, when I'm talking to you."

"What are you talkin' about?" Linc asked.

"I want to get close enough to give you all a chance to change your minds," Clint said. "The rest of the town doesn't have to hear our conversation."

"What conversation?" Linc demanded. "I'm not here to talk."

"Well, I am," Clint said. "I want to talk to you before you make me kill you."

Pete asked out of the corner of his mouth, "Why ain't he scared, Linc?" It was a question Clint just barely heard. Apparently, Pete thought that one lone man facing three should be showing fear.

Clint stopped walking then, close enough for his purposes.

"Look at Pete, Linc," Clint said. "He's so scared he's not going to be of any use to you."

"Shut up!" Pete shouted.

"And what about Hank, there? Is he any good with a gun? 'Cause he's sweating, too."

"Shut up, Adams." This time it was Linc. "I don't even need them to finish you. I can do it myself."

"Why are they here, then?" Clint asked. "Why sacrifice them?"

"What's he mean, sacrifice?" Pete asked, confused.

"Let's let them walk away, so I don't have to kill them, too."

"Linc wants to share this with us," Hank said.

"Are you boys that close that you want to share dying?" Clint asked. "I never had a brother, so I don't know if they feel that close."

"You're the one who's going to die," Linc said.

"I'm giving the three of you one last chance," Clint said. "Any of you who wants to walk away and live, do it now."

"Stand fast!" Linc said to his brothers. "Don't let him push you."

"Pete? Hank? Is it a good day to die?"

He watched as both Pete's and Hank's eyes shifted nervously. They also shifted their feet and flexed their hands, and for a moment Hank tried to dry his gun hand on his shirt, leaving a wet smear.

"What's it going to be, boys?"

Before either of the nervous brothers could respond, Linc said, "Damn you!" and drew his gun.

Grace flinched when she heard the shots, then turned and came half out of her seat. She stopped herself from running to the window. Dan was looking out over the doors, along with Clive.

"What happened?" she demanded. "What happened?"

Dan turned and looked at her.

"He got them," he said. "He got all three."

She hadn't counted the shots, but it had sounded like more than three to her. It had sounded like dozens of shots to her.

Dan came away from the doors and walked over to her.

"He took Linc first, square in the middle, putting him down like a dog," Dan said. "Then he shot Hank clean through, before he could even clear leather. And Pete, his hands were so wet with sweat he couldn't even grab his gun."

"And Clint shot him, too?"

Dan nodded.

"Are they all dead?"

Clive answered that question.

"They're checking the bodies now."

"Who's they?" she asked.

"All of a sudden the street is filled with people," he said. "It looks like . . . Linc is dead, and Hank, too, but Pete . . . they're carrying Pete, probably to the doctor's."

"So he didn't kill all three," she said.

"He shot all three," Dan said, "quick and clean as you please, he outdrew all three. I ain't never seen anything like it."

Grace closed her eyes and asked, "Why would you want to?"

FIVE

Clint rolled over in bed and looked down at Grace Whitney, who was sleeping next to him. The sunlight coming in the window made her look as if she were aglow. Her blond hair looked gold, and the light, downy hairs on her arm and back seemed to be on fire.

He put his hand on her back, ran it along her spine, down to where her buttocks swelled. He ran his hand over her ass, then one finger along the crease between her buttocks. She moaned and moved a bit, grinding her crotch into the bed. He leaned over and kissed her between the shoulders, then along the spine. He ran his tongue along the crease, then kissed each cheek gently.

"Oh," she said.

"What?"

"You've made me all wet."

"Really?" he asked. "Turn over."

She did, bringing her big, solid breasts into view, and her blond bush, which also reflected the light from the window.

"Wow," he said.

"I like to hear that when you're looking at me," she said, stretching her body. "What did I do to deserve it?"

"The sun does amazing things to your body."

17

She looked down at herself with sleepy eyes and said, "That's because I'm blond."

"Yes," he said, "you certainly are."

He kissed her belly, and then lower, until he could smell her wetness.

"Mmm," he said, "you smell great."

"That's my woman smell," she said playfully.

"And I love your belly."

It wasn't flat, like a lot of younger women. He liked that it was soft.

"It's poochy," she said. "It pooches out."

As far back as he could remember he recalled only one other woman using that word to describe her belly. It seemed appropriate now, as it had then.

"I like poochy," he said. "I like my women with meat on their bones."

"Well, then," she said, "you're in luck, because you've got one."

He cupped her crotch for a moment, just to tease her, then probed her wetness with his fingers, causing her to squirm.

"Oh," she said, jumping a bit, "it's like you've got lightning in your fingers."

He stroked the lips of her vagina gently, enjoying how slick it made his fingers, then he slid one finger inside of her, into her wetness and her heat.

"Mmm," she said, lifting her hips into his pressure. "Oh."

He slid his finger in and out, then slid two fingers into her, moved them around a bit.

"Oh," she said, pushing him away, "I want to do you first."

He didn't argue. He lay down on his back and she got down between his legs. His penis was hard and pulsing already, having stiffened the moment he smelled her.

She licked the head of his penis and sucked it just enough to wet it thoroughly, then began to lick his shaft lovingly. She held him in her hands while she worked her way back to the top, and then suddenly engulfed him in her hot mouth.

"Jesus," he said, lifting his hips as she began to ride him wetly. He reached for her head, held it briefly, then stroked her shoulders, her neck, and reached beneath her to touch her breasts.

"Stop it," she said, releasing him momentarily and slapping his hands away. "Just lie back and enjoy it."

"Yes, ma'am."

He settled in to do just that, and she worked on him for what seemed a very long time, sucking him, stroking him with her hand, touching little places on his body that were sensitive before taking him in her mouth again and sucking him long and easy, bringing him to that place that was the absolute best, that place just before the release, when he seemed to be most sensitive of all, when it seemed like that release might never come, even though it was building up, building, building . . . and then not building anymore.

SIX

Clint left Grace in his hotel room, in his bed, continuing her night's sleep. She didn't have to be at work until late in the afternoon. He hadn't had the heart to tell her that he'd only be spending one more night in town, and then he'd be leaving. Killing someone always seemed to ruin a town for him.

He went across the street to the doctor's office to check on Pete Jensen. The doctor, a grizzled veteran of many towns in the West who had settled in Hampton, looked up from his desk.

"Doc," Clint said.

"Mr. Adams."

"How's the patient?"

"He lasted the night," the doctor said, sitting back in his chair. "He'll pull through."

"Can I see him?"

Doctor Ed Cassidy frowned at the question.

"Why? You killed his brothers, and almost killed him. Why would you want to see him? Why would he want to see you?"

"Is he strong enough for me to talk to him?" Clint asked, ignoring the man's questions.

21

"Sure," Cassidy said, "and I suppose he's in no condition to refuse, is he?"

The doctor got up from his desk.

"Come with me."

The doctor had a facility at his disposal that almost qualified as a hospital. He had a large room in the back with several beds in it, and the only one occupied at the moment was the one with Pete Jensen in it.

"There he is," the doctor said. "I'll be at my desk."

"Okay."

The doctor left the room and closed the door behind him. Clint walked across the room to the bed Pete Jensen was lying in. Jensen was lying with his eyes open, and his head turned the other way. Clint knew his bullet had not missed the young man's heart by much.

"Pete?"

Jensen turned his head and his eyes widened when he saw Clint.

"What do you want?" he demanded. "You come to finish the job? I don't have a gun in bed with me."

"You and your brothers came after me, Pete," Clint said. "There's no way I'm going to feel any guilt over what happened."

"And I should?"

Clint spread his hands.

"This all happened because you got drunk and belligerent. You made me take your guns away from you and your brother."

"You made a fool of me—fools of us."

"And that was so bad?" Clint asked. "That was worth dying over? Having your brothers die?"

"Linc said he could take you."

"Then why did he need you and your brother?"

"He was . . . sharing the glory."

"Pete, you're a young man," Clint said. "There's no glory in killing a man."

Jensen turned his head away.

"I don't want to talk to you."

"I'm leaving town tomorrow."

Jensen looked at Clint and sneered.

"Gonna leave before I get back on my feet?"

Clint frowned.

"Are you thinking of coming after me, Pete?"

"I got to."

"No, you don't," Clint said. "You were scared yesterday, facing me with your brothers there next to you. How do you think you'll do alone?"

"I'm gonna kill you."

"You're kidding yourself," Clint said. "I shot you once, don't make me kill you."

"I'm gonna kill *you*," Pete Jensen said very deliberately.

Clint shook his head.

"It's not going to happen, Pete."

Jensen looked away again.

"Get out, Adams."

"I'm going, Pete," Clint said, "but once I leave town, don't follow me. I'm warning you."

Jensen didn't say anything, and Clint went back out to the doctor's office.

"Who's paying your bill, Doc?" Clint asked.

"I haven't the faintest idea."

Clint dropped some money on the desk.

"That cover it?"

"Sure," the doctor said, "but why would you shoot a man and then pay his medical bill?"

"I didn't want to shoot him, Doc," Clint said. "I didn't want to shoot any of them." He walked to the door. "Take care of him, and try to talk him out of coming after me."

"That's not part of my job," the doctor said. "Besides, you killed his brothers. What would you expect him to do?"

Clint stared at the doctor for a few moments, then

shook his head and walked out of the office. He was outside when the thought occurred to him that there was no
way Pete Jensen could face him and kill him—not alone,
anyway.

SEVEN

"You want to know *what*?" Sheriff Willard asked Clint just minutes later.

"I want to know if Pete Jensen has any other family," Clint said again.

"Well, his paw up and left years ago, and his maw died a couple of years ago."

"What about cousins?"

"Oh, sure," Willard said, "Pete and Hank and Linc, they had lots of cousins. Uh, I guess I mean Pete's got a lot of cousins now."

"Do they live around here?"

"Naw," the sheriff said, "they're mountain folk."

Clint knew that mountain folk were real clannish. If Pete went to them and told them what had happened they'd likely ride with him.

"How many cousins?"

"I don't rightly know," Willard said, stroking his chin. "Half a dozen, maybe more—more for sure if you count the females."

"I see."

"You worried he's gonna come after you?"

"Yes, I am."

"You afraid?"

"I don't relish the idea of having to wipe out a whole family," Clint said. "You'd do the boy good to talk to him, Sheriff. Talk him out of coming after me."

"You killed his brothers," Willard said. "What do you expect him to do?"

"Never mind," Clint said, and left the office.

The next person he talked to about Pete Jensen was Dan, the bartender at the saloon.

"You killed his brothers," Dan said, "wha—"

"That's all I've been hearing," Clint said, cutting him off. "Do you have a brother, Dan?"

"Yeah, I do. He's up in Idaho, somewheres."

"And if somebody killed him, would you go after the killer?"

"Hell no."

"Why not?"

"I hate my brother," Dan said, "and he hates me. Somebody killed him I'd give him a medal."

"I guess all brothers are different, huh?" Clint asked.

"I guess so. I tell you what, though."

"What?"

"I think if you had killed Pete and Hank, Linc wouldn't be after you for it."

"He wouldn't?"

"He was gettin' tired of takin' care of those boys," Dan said. "Of course, he'd still come after you, but it would be to make a name for himself, not because you killed his brothers."

"I see. Let me ask you something."

"What?"

"Is there anybody in this town Pete Jensen might listen to?"

"For what?"

"To tell him not to come after me."

Dan thought a moment, then shook his head.

"No."

"What about a girl?"

"Oh, sure, Pete's got a girl."

"Who is she?"

"Her name's Sheila Dillon," the bartender said. "Her father runs the feed and grain. Hey, maybe you can talk to her."

"Maybe I will. Thanks, Dan."

"Sure thing. Hey, are you gonna be leavin'?"

"Tomorrow."

"Can't say as I blame you," he said. "Come back in later and I'll buy you a beer on the house."

"I'll be in," Clint promised.

EIGHT

Clint went over to the feed and grain store. Behind the counter was a young girl, maybe seventeen, with long brown hair and the kind of face most people would call "horsey." She was short, and so thin her arms looked like all bone and no meat.

"Sheila?"

She looked up at him.

"Yes? Do I know you?"

"I don't think so," he said. "My name's Clint Adams."

"Oh," she said. "You're the one shot the Jensen boys."

"That's right," Clint said, "after they came after me."

"I know that."

"Oh," he said. "I thought you'd be upset, you know, about Pete?"

"Why should I be?" she asked. "Pete Jensen don't mean nothin' to me."

"I thought you were his girl."

"I was," she said, "until he and his brothers decided to go after you. I told him I wouldn't have nothin' to do with him if he did that."

"Why'd you do that?"

"I expected him to get killed."

"And now that he's not dead?"

"I still don't want nothin' to do with him," she said. "Pete's stupid. It was stupid of him to follow Linc and go after you. And I'll tell you another thing."

"What's that?"

"He's gonna be stupid when he gets back on his feet and comes after you for killing his brothers."

"That's what I wanted to talk to you about," Clint said. "I want you to talk him out of it."

"Can't," she said, shaking her head.

"Why not?"

"I ain't talkin' to him."

"Not even to save his life?"

"Can't," she said again.

He was about to say something when a man came out of a door behind the counter. He was tall, rawboned, and had the same shaped face his daughter had.

"Who's this?" he demanded.

"This is the fella shot the Jensens."

"Hmph," the man said, "did this town a favor, you ask me. What's he doin' here?"

Clint wondered why the man didn't ask him these questions directly.

"He wants me to talk Pete Jensen out of goin' after him when he gets back on his feet."

"You stay away from Pete Jensen, girl, you hear?" the man blustered. "You ain't too big for me to tan your hide if you don't."

"Yes, Papa."

"I'll be in the office, doin' the books," he said, and disappeared through another door without once having looked at Clint.

"I think I see why you can't talk to Pete."

"Pa says Pete Jensen's worthless, and he's right," the girl said.

"I see."

"He comes after you," she said, "he ain't gonna do it alone."

"I understand he's got a lot of cousins in the mountains."

"Five," she said, "eleven if you count the girls."

"Five."

"That's right, and they're all worthless," she said.

"Well," Clint said, "I guess you can't help me, Sheila. Thanks for talking to me, though."

He started for the door.

"Mister?"

He turned.

"Yes?"

"You gonna kill them all?"

"I sure hope not, Sheila," he said. "I sure hope not."

NINE

Later that evening Clint was in the saloon. Grace was walking around, working, and Clint was working on his free beer, sitting at Clive Lovejoy's table.

"Are you leaving tomorrow?" Clive asked.

"Yes."

"Tell Grace yet?"

"No."

"She'll be disappointed."

"I know."

"I can't blame you, though," Lovejoy said. "I'm thinking of leaving, myself."

"Why?"

"I've had enough of this town."

"You'll have to sell out."

"That won't be difficult."

"Where will you go?" Clint asked. "Back to England?"

"No," Lovejoy said, shaking his head, "San Francisco. That's where I belong. In San Francisco, owning and running a place ten times the size of this one."

"There are plenty of them there."

"Have you been there?"

"Many times."

"Then you know," Lovejoy said. "A man like me would thrive there."

"You know," Clint said, "I believe you're right, Clive."

That seemed to please the saloon owner.

"You know," he said, "I think I'll buy you a beer on the house."

Clint held up his empty mug and said, "This one was on the house."

"Then you shall have another, dear boy," Clive said. "You shall have another."

After a few beers Clint decided to go to the livery while it was still afternoon and arrange to have Duke ready in the morning. While he was there he took the opportunity to check on the horse's soundness himself, and found him in fine health.

For as long as Clint and Duke had been together—and it had been a long time—the only serious illness that had befallen the horse was being shot. The big gelding had survived that and had not had a serious ailment since.

"We're going to get going tomorrow, big fella," Clint said, stroking the gelding's neck. "Time to get going again."

Clint decided they'd head for Texas, and maybe continue on to Labyrinth, where his friend Rick Hartman lived. The town was a safe haven for Clint and Duke, and Clint felt he needed one. Not because Pete Jensen and his cousins might be after him, but because he had been away from there for a while this time, on the trail for a while, and he was tired.

"See you tomorrow, big guy," he said to Duke, and left the livery.

He was torn between the saloon and the hotel, and decided on the hotel. Suddenly, he felt he needed about an hour alone in his room, maybe even to sleep.

Was he getting old, starting to need a nap late in the day?

Hell, what was one nap?

"Where did Clint go?" Grace asked Clive.

"I don't think I could say for sure, dear girl," Lovejoy answered.

She sat down with her boss.

"He's leaving tomorrow, isn't he?"

"Did he tell you that?"

"He didn't have to," she said. "I can feel it."

"Grace," he said, looking at her, "I'm going to sell this place and go to San Francisco. Will you come with me?"

"What did you have in mind, Clive?" she asked suspiciously.

"Nothing like that, dear girl," he assured her. "Get your mind out of the gutter. I want to go to San Francisco and run a place—or own a place—there. Will you come and work for me?"

"And leave all this?" she asked sarcastically. "When do we leave?"

"Quite soon, actually," he said. "I've been thinking about this for some time, and I believe I might be able to get the bank to buy this place from me. We wouldn't have to wait around for a buyer."

"That sounds good to me," she said. "I was starting to get tired of this town, anyway."

"So was I."

She stared at her boss for a moment, then said, "Thank you, Clive."

"Thank you, my girl," he said. "You have always been dependable, and I think I shall need a dependable right hand in San Francisco."

"Of course," she said, "a dependable right hand gets paid a lot more than a saloon girl, huh?"

Clive Lovejoy smiled and said, "I think we shall cross that particular bridge when we come to it, Grace, eh?"

TEN

When the knock came at the door Clint couldn't believe it. It was dark outside and he had slept for hours, rather than an hour.

He got out of bed and staggered to the door. When he opened it, a worried Grace stepped inside.

"Are you all right?" she asked, closing the door.

"I'm fine," he said. "I just . . . fell asleep."

He sat on the bed and she sat next to him.

"What's wrong?"

"Nothing."

"Something is."

He hesitated, then said, "I'm leaving tomorrow."

"I know."

"Clive told you?"

She shook her head.

"Nobody had to tell me."

"You're too smart for your own good."

"Smart enough to know that's not what's bothering you."

"No," he said, "it's not."

"It's killing those men, isn't it?"

"To a small degree," he said. "Actually, it's more the live one that bothers me."

"Pete?" she said. "You don't have to worry about Pete Jensen, do you?"

"I'm worried I'll have to kill him," he said. "He's going to come after me, Grace, and he'll probably bring help with him. I understand he's got a lot of cousins."

"I heard that."

"I don't look forward to trying to kill a whole family."

"What makes you think he'll be able to find you?"

"I'm not exactly unknown," he said. "I don't think I'll be that hard to locate."

"So hide someplace."

"I can't do that, either."

"Why not?"

"Because . . . I can't just hide the rest of my life," he said. "I would never be able to live that way."

"Then what will you do?"

"I don't know."

"Where are you going to head tomorrow?"

"Probably Texas."

"Texas is a big place."

"I know."

She shifted so that her shoulder was touching his and her hip was pressed to his.

"I'm leaving, too."

"To go where?"

"San Francisco."

He looked surprised.

"With Clive?"

"Anything wrong with that?" she asked defensively. "It's a business arrangement."

"No, no," he said, "nothing's wrong with that. I think you and Clive make a good team."

"Maybe you'll come to San Francisco one day?"

He smiled.

"I go there a lot," he said.

"That's great," she said. "Then we'll see each other again."

"I'm sure of it."

"Unless . . ."

"Unless what?"

She looked down at her hands in her lap.

"Unless you already have a woman there."

"No one in particular, Grace. I'll be happy to stop in and see you whenever I'm in San Francisco."

She looked at him and smiled.

"That's wonderful."

"Are you hungry?" he asked. "Suddenly I'm hungry."

"I'm starved."

"Let's go get something to eat someplace," he said. "It's still early enough—speaking of which, what are you doing here this early? Aren't you supposed to still be working?"

"Clive gave me the rest of the night off," she said, "to say good-bye to you."

"Well," he said, taking her hand, "that sounds promising."

He kissed her, but as the kiss deepened and heated up he pulled away, got up, and tugged her to her feet.

"But first, we have to eat."

ELEVEN

Clint awoke the next morning and looked down at Grace, lying next to him. She was lying on her back and, in repose, her face totally relaxed, she looked almost like a young girl—except she wasn't. She was a beautiful woman in her thirties who had been through a lot in her life. He hoped she would find the happiness she deserved in San Francisco—maybe even with Clive Lovejoy.

Pete Jensen awoke abruptly that morning. He'd had the dream again, facing Clint Adams in the street, only this time Adams shot him first, and several times. As he was falling he saw Adams shoot both his brothers, and he knew he was dead . . . until he woke up in a sweat.

Jensen knew that he'd be having this same dream for years unless he did something about it. He had to kill Clint Adams, and he knew he couldn't do it by himself. He wouldn't even be able to do it from hiding, because he was a lousy shot. He was going to have to round up his cousins, tell them what had happened, and then decide what to do. Maybe one of them would just be able to shoot Adams from a rooftop. Kyle was a good shot, maybe he could do it. Or John-Boy. Or even Amanda. She was a hell of a shot, for a girl.

41

He didn't care how it got done; Clint Adams had to die for what he'd done—and then the dream would go away.

Pete Jensen simply could not stand to die like that every night for the rest of his life.

Clive Lovejoy was alone in his room that morning, dressing in his finest suit. He was going to go to the bank and make a deal for the saloon, even if he had to take less than it was worth. It was simply time to move on. San Francisco was calling.

He wondered about Grace Whitney. Once they were away from here, and she was away from Clint Adams, he wondered if he'd have any chance to make her fall in love with him. Once they got set up in San Francisco, he'd start working on her. Little by little, maybe he could win her over.

But first things first. He tightened his tie and approved of the way he looked in the mirror. He had a deal to close.

Grace kept her eyes closed, even though she knew Clint was looking down at her. She was not ready to open them, because that would mean it was time for him to go, time to say good-bye.

She just wasn't ready for that yet.

"Grace?"

Reluctantly, she finally opened her eyes. He'd called her name twice.

"Good morning," he said.

"Is it?"

"Time for me to go."

"I know."

He kissed her, and moved away from her. She watched as he dressed.

"When do you think you'll be leaving?" he asked her.

"I don't know," she said. "Clive said he thought he could make a deal with the bank to buy the saloon."

"That would be convenient," he said. "You wouldn't have to wait around for a buyer."

"That's what he said."

He finished dressing, packed up his things—his saddle-bags, his bedroll—and picked up his rifle.

"I think I'll stay here," she said. "I don't want to say good-bye in the street."

"Grace—"

"Just go," she said. "We'll see each other sometime, in San Francisco."

"Good luck."

"Yes," she said, "good luck to you, too."

He left and she turned over in bed, moving to his side. She would stay there until his warmth was gone.

TWELVE

Two weeks later Clint was lamenting the fact that he had just recently been pondering Duke's durability. They were in the town of Chester, Texas, just over the border from Oklahoma. They had been there for over a week while Duke was recovering from an injury he'd sustained when he stepped into a chuckhole. Of course, it wasn't entirely his fault that he stepped into the hole—Clint could have spotted it and steered him away—and the injury certainly couldn't be attributed to illness.

Still, it was ironic that, while in Hampton, Missouri, he had been thinking about the gelding's soundness, and here they were waiting for him to heal.

Maybe it was his fault for thinking about it in the first place.

Chester, Texas, wasn't much of a town. In fact, it wasn't much more than a way station. It had a saloon that also rented rooms upstairs, and a few other buildings, but it didn't have a sheriff, or a jail, or—according to the bartender—any crime.

"No need for a jail when you don't got no crime," the man said.

"I guess not," Clint said.

There was nothing to do but sit and drink and think in Chester. There were no women in the saloon, and there was no whorehouse. Clint spent the days sitting in the saloon, and the evenings playing poker for nickels with three of the locals.

Actually, if it wasn't for the poker, he probably would have gone crazy by now.

Clint still didn't know the names of his poker buddies. They were just faces who came into the saloon each night, sat down, and played. They didn't even know his name, and that was fine with him. If they found out who he was, the word would spread very quickly in a small town like Chester. Luckily, he hadn't even had to give his name to rent a room, just a dollar a day.

It occurred to him that he was in a sort of limbo. Nobody knew him, and no one knew where he was. He decided a little boredom never hurt anybody.

Things could have been a lot worse.

THIRTEEN

Pete Jensen left the doctor's office ten days after he'd been shot. This was against the doctor's wishes, but Jensen didn't want Clint Adams getting too far away.

It was still three days later, though, before his cousins rode into town in response to his telegram.

He watched them as they rode toward where he was sitting, in front of the hotel. There was Vern, Evan, John-Boy, and Kyle, the oldest. Amanda was also there, along with Dave, the second youngest to John-Boy.

They lined up in front of the hotel and looked down at Pete.

"Can you ride?" Kyle asked.

With Linc gone, Kyle was the oldest of the cousins. In fact, the oldest male Jensen left.

"I can ride."

"Well," Kyle said, "get your horse, then, and let's get after this fella. We got work to do back home."

Pete stood up.

"Kyle, I ain't stoppin' until he's dead."

Kyle leaned over and spat out a wad of tobacco juice before answering.

"We ain't stoppin' either, Cousin," Kyle said. "Now you get a move on and get set on your horse."

"It's at the livery," Pete said. "I'll be ready in five minutes."

As Pete hurried away, John-Boy asked, "This town got a whorehouse?"

"He said five minutes, John-Boy," Evan said. "That enough time fer you?"

"Shit," John-Boy said, "I cain't even get my pants off in five minutes, my dick is so long."

Amanda, who but for Kyle was the oldest, leaned over and punched John-Boy in the face, knocking him from his saddle.

"What'd you do that fer?" he demanded from the seat of his pants in the dirt. He was probing his jaw to see if it was broken. Amanda wasn't that big, but she was mean, and packed a punch.

"I don't want to hear about your dick, John-Boy," Amanda said, "I tole you that before."

"Okay, okay," he said, picking himself up from the ground.

She had plenty of dicks back home, he thought as he remounted, what the hell was wrong with talking about his? He was her own brother, wasn't he? What the hell was wrong with that?

Then he remembered that she was the only one in the group who had ever really seen his dick, and she could tell the others he was lying about his size. He decided he'd better be nice to her so she wouldn't snitch on him.

"I'm sorry, Amanda," he said. "I didn't mean to offend you."

"I accept your apology," Amanda said, looking at her younger brother fondly. Of all of them he was the youngest, the dumbest, and the one she loved the best—though she never let any of them know it, least of all him.

John-Boy looked over at Dave and smiled. The smile told his brother that he figured he'd gotten over on their sister. Dave didn't talk much, so he just smiled back and shook his head.

John-Boy was the only one who didn't know that there was just no way to get over on Amanda.

Amanda had changed John-Boy's diapers more than once when he was little, and she had even seen him without his pants a time or two in the past few years. She knew he had a little bitty dick, which was why he was lying about it all the time. She also didn't think that her little brother had ever gotten his dick wet yet. That was something else he lied about.

"Let's stop bickerin' and get over to the livery," Kyle said.

"Sure, Kyle," John-Boy said.

She knew he was as scared of Kyle as he had ever been of Linc. Amanda was the only one who was never scared of either one of them.

She was kind of scary herself, though.

Kyle led the family over to the livery as Pete was walking out with his horse.

"We got some supplies," he said to his cousin, "but we figure to travel light to make up some ground."

"That's just fine," Pete said as he mounted up.

"Where was he headed?" Kyle asked.

"I heard Texas."

"Then that's where we'll start."

"Texas is a big place," Evan said. "We could be away from home a long time."

"This is family business, Evan," Kyle said to his brother. "Don't matter how long it takes, it got to get done."

"The longer we stay away from chores," John-Boy said, "the better I like it."

Vern laughed, but Kyle ignored the remark. Seeing this, Vern stopped laughing. Kyle rode up alongside of Pete.

"Tell me somethin', Pete."

"What, Kyle?"

"This Adams, he outdrew the three of you clean?"

"He did."

"Shot Linc dead, huh?"

"He did that, too—and Hank."

Kyle spat a stream of tobacco. Hank was no hand with a gun, he knew that. Still, drawing on three men and plugging them all, that was impressive.

"And he didn't get shot?"

"Not a scratch."

Kyle spat again, then wiped some brown spittle off his chin with his sleeve.

"Always did fancy myself better than Linc with a gun, but it would never do for two family members to face each other," he said. "I reckon I got me a chance to prove it now."

"By taking Adams?"

Kyle nodded.

"He's fast, Kyle," Pete said, "awful fast."

"I'm faster," Kyle said without hesitation. "Ain't nobody faster than me."

"Except maybe me," Amanda said with a grin.

Kyle turned his hooded eyes on his sister.

"You're a better shot, Mandy," he said, "but I'm faster."

"If I could reach you," she said, looking at him across Evan's horse, which was between them, "I'd punch you out of your saddle. I tole you never to call me Mandy."

"Yeah," Kyle said, showing tobacco stained teeth in a smile, "you did."

FOURTEEN

After he was in Chester two weeks, Clint realized that, little by little, he was making some money. His room was only a dollar a day, and his meals not much more than that. As long as he was in the saloon there were sandwiches and hard-boiled eggs on the bar. A man could live on that—and beer.

With what he was winning at nickel poker he was making more than he was laying out, day by day.

He was also treating Duke's leg himself, although the best treatment for the big horse was simply rest. He was only paying two bits a day for a stall at the run-down livery.

Clint entered the Chester saloon—which had no name, since it was the only saloon in town—and ordered a beer from the bartender, who also owned the place. His name was Leo Vincey.

"Starting a third week," Vincey said. "Maybe you're likin' it here some?"

Clint had just been out stretching his legs and hadn't seen anything to like.

"I value my horse too much to try to push him too soon," Clint said. "I'll stay as long as it takes for him to heal properly."

"Can't blame you for that," Vincey said. "He's a good-lookin' animal."

"He is that," Clint said, "but he's getting up in years, and he needs more time to heal."

"Got another stranger in town today," Vincey said by way of conversation. "Yep. Put him in three, down the hall from you."

"What's his reason for being here?"

"Just passing through, he says," Vincey answered.

"Maybe he plays poker," Clint said. "We could use some new blood in the game."

Clint realized he sounded as if he lived in Chester and he shuddered. Even though he was making money this was no place to settle down. It had been some time since he had even seen a good-looking woman. Fondly, he thought back on Grace Whitney in Hampton. He wondered if she and Clive Lovejoy had made it to San Francisco by now.

"Speak of the devil," Vincey said.

Clint turned and saw a man coming down the stairs from the second floor. He was in his thirties, built rangy, wearing weather-worn clothes and a matching gun and holster.

"Can I get a beer?" the man asked, stepping up to the bar.

"Comin' up."

"Howdy," he said to Clint.

"Hello."

"You the other stranger in town the bartender was telling me about?"

"That's right."

"The name's Pardo," the man said, extending his hand, "William Pardo."

"William?" Clint asked. "Not Bill?"

"I prefer William."

Clint shook the man's hand and said, "My name is Clint."

The man didn't push for a last name while they shook hands. Vincey returned with the man's beer and set it on the bar.

"What brings you to this town?" Pardo asked.

"My horse came up lame a few miles from here," Clint said. "I'm letting him heal."

"That big black in the livery?"

"That's him."

"Fine-lookin' animal."

"Thanks. What brings you here?"

"I'm just passing through," Pardo said. "I just need a place to set a spell, maybe spend a couple of nights in a real bed."

"A bed is about all this town has to offer," Clint said. "No women?"

Clint shook his head grimly and said, "No women."

"You play poker, Mr. Pardo?" Leo Vincey asked, cutting in.

"Some," Pardo said, looking at the bartender, and then back to Clint. "Why, is there a game?"

"Just a nickel game," Clint said. "Some of the locals play every night."

"You play?"

"I've been sitting in to kill time."

"Poker sounds like a good way to kill time," Pardo said. "Mind if I sit in?"

"Could always use a fifth hand," Clint said.

"Think the others would mind?"

"Can't see why they would," Clint said. "Fresh money's always welcome."

"Even fresh nickels, huh?" Pardo asked.

"Even fresh nickels."

Clint and Pardo continued to make small talk while they finished their beers, but Clint couldn't shake the feeling that he had met the man somewhere before. He didn't know if Pardo knew who he was, and asking the man some questions might entail offering up his own last name. Clint decided to sit tight and just see if something came to him.

FIFTEEN

As Clint had predicted, the other players did not object to a fifth hand.

"Maybe it'll change your friend's luck," one of them said.

"Oh, we're not friends," Pardo said, "we just met today."

"It don't matter," another man said, "maybe you'll change his luck, anyway."

As it turned out, he didn't. In fact, Pardo was a very bad poker player and only took one hand during the first two hours.

"I need a beer," Pardo said. "Losing makes a man thirsty. Anything for anybody else?"

"No," Clint said, and the others shook their heads.

"You in?" the dealer asked.

"I'm in," Pardo said. "I'll be back with a beer."

When Pardo returned there were two cards waiting for him. The one everyone could see was an ace. When he looked at his hole card, he saw that this was an ace, as well.

"Your bet," the dealer said.

Pardo sipped his beer and put it down carefully on his left, between him and Clint.

"I'll bet a nickel," he said.

"Call," Clint said, and everyone else saw the bet, as well.

The dealer came out with everyone's third card, and Pardo had a pair of aces showing.

"Two nickels," he said.

Clint had a pair of tens on the table and stayed in. Because it was a five-card game, the other players all went out with mismatched cards on the table.

"You and me, huh, Clint?" Pardo asked.

"I guess so."

Clint examined the other players to see if any of them reacted to the sound of his first name. This would be the first time any of them had heard it—if they heard it. None of them acted as if they had.

The dealer gave them each their fourth card. Pardo got a ten, and Clint caught a king.

"Your ten," Pardo said.

"Bet your aces," the dealer said.

"Three nickels," Pardo said.

"I'll call."

"You must have three tens," Pardo said, "but you can't catch the fourth."

"Last card," the dealer said.

Pardo got a four, but Clint got another king.

"Two pair bets," the dealer said.

"Five nickels," Clint said.

"Your five," Pardo said without hesitation, "and five more."

Clint felt sure Pardo had three aces, but he had another king in the hole to complete a full house.

"I reraise," he said.

"And I raise again," Pardo said, looking satisfied with himself.

"I'm going to call."

"Ha!" Pardo said. "Three aces. Beat 'em."

Clint turned over the king he had in the hole.

"Full house," the dealer said. "He did beat 'em."

"Son of a bitch," Pardo said, without rancor. "That was the best hand I had all night."

"Maybe it's time to quit," Clint said.

"Aw, why?" Pardo asked. "I'm just passing the time. Come on, let's play."

"Suit yourself," Clint said, raking in his pot of nickels.

The next dealer gathered up the cards, shuffled them, and said, "Comin' out."

SIXTEEN

When the game broke up Clint went to the bar for a beer. Pardo paused at the table to talk with the other men.

"A beer," Clint said to Vincey.

"Think anybody can really be that bad a poker player?" the bartender asked as he set Clint's beer down in front of him.

"I guess so," Clint said. "Why would somebody play that bad on purpose?"

"Why would anybody bother to play when they play that bad?" Vincey asked.

"Just killin' time, Leo," Clint said.

"I suppose so."

Pardo came up next to Clint abruptly and said, "Buy me a beer with your winnings?"

"Sure," Clint said. He looked at Vincey, who nodded and went off to get it.

"You play poker real well," Pardo said.

"You don't," Clint said. "I remember where I saw you before."

"Oh?"

"Tannerville, wasn't it?"

Pardo looked away.

"You played poker real bad for two days before you

59

came back the third day and took everybody's money. They all thought you were real lucky that day, didn't they?''

"I guess they did," Pardo said sheepishly.

"Why try to hustle a nickel game, Pardo?" Clint asked.

"Maybe because you were in it?" the man answered.

Vincey came with the beer, and both Clint and Pardo fell silent.

"What do you mean by that?"

Pardo sipped his beer.

"Anybody else in this town know who you are, or am I the only one, Clint?"

"Well, only you, if you're right."

"Oh, I'm right," Pardo said. "I stayed out of that game in Tannerville while you were in it, remember?"

"Yes," Clint said, "I do remember that, now."

"So tell me," Pardo said, "what are you doing in a nickel-ante game in a penny-ante town?"

"I told you," Clint said. "Waiting for my horse to heal."

"That's on the level?"

Clint nodded.

"So there's no big game in the offing?"

"Not that I know of," Clint said. "Not unless you can get these fellas to up the ante to a dime—uh, but if you do that, wait until I leave, huh?"

"Don't worry," Pardo said. "A nickel game is the biggest game I want to sit in with you. See, I know my limitations. You're a better player than I am."

Clint looked at Pardo and said, "Are you trying to con me, Pardo?"

"Hell, no," Pardo said. "What kind of an idiot would I be to try and con . . . the Gunsmith?" He lowered his voice at the end of his sentence.

"I don't know," Clint said. "How many kinds of idiot are there?"

"I'm not stupid, Clint."

"There's nothing brewing here, Pardo," Clint said. "I'm just stuck here for a while."

"Sure, sure," Pardo said. "Maybe I'll just stick around for a while, too."

"Suit yourself."

"Maybe I can even help you."

"With what?"

"Well . . . you ever heard of a family called the Jensens?"

Clint paused with his beer halfway to his mouth.

"What about them?"

"I hear there's a bunch of them on the prowl," Pardo said. "Cousins, or brothers? Somethin' like that?"

"Most likely cousins."

"I hear they're looking for you."

"Where'd you hear that?"

"I keep my ears open."

"What else do you hear?"

"I hear they're headed this way."

"How far out?"

"Two, maybe three days," Pardo said. "Of course, they might just bypass this place."

"You didn't."

"No, I didn't," Pardo said, "but then, I was telling the truth."

"About what?"

"I really was looking for a real bed for a couple of nights."

"Uh-huh."

"And you?"

Clint sipped his beer and put the mug down.

"I was telling the truth, too, Pardo," Clint said. "I'm stuck here."

"Why are the Jensens after you?"

Clint didn't see any reason not to tell the man the story of what had happened in Hampton. Pardo was a good listener and didn't interrupt once.

"I've heard of Linc Jensen," he said when Clint was done.

"Have you heard of any of the other Jensens?"

"Just one."

"Who would that be?"

"Kyle," Pardo said. "He'd be the oldest, now that Linc's dead."

"You seem to know a lot about the family," Clint said.

"Just what I've heard," Pardo said. "See, I'm from Missouri, originally. Some of them are from Missouri, and some are from Arkansas."

"What else do you know about them?"

"They've got a mighty strong sense of family," Pardo said. "When one of them is slighted, or hurt, they all band together."

Clint nursed his beer.

"Of course," Pardo said, "you killed one of them."

"Two."

"Right," he said, "two, and injured a third. They'll hunt you down, Clint, or grow old trying."

"I guess they will," Clint said. "What kind of help were you offering? Standing with me?"

"Well . . . we don't know each other well enough for that, do we?" Pardo asked. "I mean, for me to risk my life like that?"

"No, I guess we don't."

"Maybe I just helped a little, just by talking, huh?" Pardo asked.

"Maybe you did."

Pardo finished his beer and added, "And maybe that's worth another beer?"

Clint nodded and waved to Vincey to bring another.

SEVENTEEN

"Where are we?" Kyle asked.

They all looked at Amanda.

"Texas," she said. These boys would all be hopelessly lost without her. The Texas wind would just blow them away if it wasn't for her.

"Where in Texas?" Kyle asked.

"We're just in Texas, Kyle," she said. "I saw a couple of signposts further back. We're near a town called Chester."

"What's there?"

"I don't know," she said, "but the sign said the population was about a hundred."

She knew that and they didn't because she could read and they couldn't.

"That ain't a town," Vern said.

"What else is around here?"

"Signal Tap is twenty miles east," Amanda said.

"And Chester?"

"About twenty miles west."

Kyle rubbed his jaw.

"He might have stopped in one of these places to stock up," she said. "Why don't we split up? You take Vern

63

and Evan and Dave and go to Signal Tap. John-Boy and I will go to Chester.''

''What about me?'' Pete asked.

''You go with Kyle.'' She looked at her older brother. ''Is that okay with you, Kyle?''

''Yeah,'' Kyle said after a moment, ''except you take Evan with you. The three of you check Chester. The rest of us will go to Signal Tap.''

''That's a good idea,'' she said. ''Where should we meet up?''

Kyle spat a stream and pondered the question.

''There's a town south of here called Jacksboro,'' she said helpfully. ''Why don't we meet there? Day after to-morrow?''

Kyle thought a moment, then said, ''We'll meet up in Jacksboro, day after tomorrow.''

''Good idea,'' Amanda said. She looked at Evan and John-Boy and said, ''Let's go.''

''Hey,'' Evan said, ''who put you in charge?''

She stared back at him.

''You want to take the lead, Evan?''

''Sure thing,'' he said. Then he looked back at her and asked, ''Where we goin', again?''

''Follow me, Evan,'' Amanda said. ''We're goin' to Chester.''

As they rode along Evan said, ''He's got to be far from here by now.''

Amanda didn't reply.

''I mean, according to Cousin Pete, he got a big head start on us. He cain't be in Chester.''

''Evan,'' Amanda said, ''we're just looking for a place he might have stopped.''

''Well, what if he stopped in Signal Tap?'' he asked. ''What if he's there and the others get to kill 'im? That ain't gonna be fair.''

''It don't matter who kills him, Evan,'' she said, ''as

long as he gets dead. Ain't that right, John-Boy?''

"That's sure right," John-Boy said, nodding.

"Aw heck, he don't count," Evan said. "He just agrees with everythin' you say."

"That's 'cause she's smart," John-Boy said, "and you ain't."

"Who says I ain't?" Evan asked. "You want to get off your horse and see who's smarter?"

"Gettin' off your horse wouldn't be too smart, Evan," Amanda said.

"Why not?" he demanded.

" 'Cause there's lots of snakes around here."

Evan's eyes widened and he looked around nervously. "Where?"

"All over the ground," Amanda said. "We're in the plains, Evan. Lots of rattlesnakes."

"Jesus!" Evan said. He hated snakes.

"Come on, Evan," John-Boy said. "You wanna get off your horse?"

"Boy, you stupid?" Evan asked. "There's snakes around here."

"There sure are," John-Boy said.

"I think we shoulda kept goin' south," Pete said to Kyle.

"We got to see if he stopped for supplies."

"He coulda stopped in Jacksboro."

"That's fifty miles."

"Kyle—"

"Who's leadin' this outfit, Pete?"

Amanda, Pete thought, but he didn't say it.

"You are, Kyle."

"Then just relax yourself," Kyle said. "We're gonna get the bastard what killed Linc and Hank. Just settle down and do like I tell you. Okay?"

"Okay, Kyle," Pete said, "sure."

EIGHTEEN

"They's a big one comin'."

Clint turned his head and looked at the old man who was sitting in a chair in front of the saloon. He'd stepped outside to get a breath of air and stretch.

"Are you talking to me?"

"I talks to anyone who'll listen, usual," the man said.

"What did you say?"

"I said they's a big one comin'."

"Big one what?"

"Sniff the air, boy," the old man said. He was seventy if he was a day, as grizzled an old coot as Clint had ever seen.

Clint sniffed the air.

"What am I smelling?" he asked. "I don't smell rain."

"T'ain't rain."

"Then what is it?"

"Wind."

Clint looked at the old man.

"How can you smell the wind?"

"I can," the old-timer said. "I smell it, and it's a big one."

"A storm?"

"A wind."

"A windstorm."

The old man looked at Clint as if he were crazy.

"There is a wind coming, I tell you," he said. "That is all I'm sayin'."

And he turned away.

Clint looked at the sky and it appeared clear. He sniffed the air again, but he'd be damned if he could smell anything.

He shrugged and went back inside.

If he'd had some company Chester wouldn't have been so bad. A woman would have been preferable, but a man to talk to would have helped pass the time. Of course, Pardo knew who he was, but Clint wasn't so sure he wanted to spend any time with the man.

He went up to his room, leaving Pardo in the saloon at the bar.

It was late when there was a knock on his door. The room was dark, and he paused to light the lamp on the table next to the bed.

"Who is it?"

"Leo Vincey," a man's voice said. "The bartender."

Clint took his gun with him to the door, because Pardo had reminded him that the Jensen family was out looking for him. Briefly he wondered if being stuck here was a good thing or a bad thing. It gave them time to catch up to him, but would they really stop here and look for him?

Clint opened the door and it was Vincey.

"What is it, Leo?"

"I was wonderin' if you could come downstairs and help me with your friend?"

"What friend?"

"You know," Vincey said, "that feller you was playin' poker with?"

Clint went to rub his face with his hand, but forgot he

was holding his gun. Vincey's eyes widened, and Clint lowered the gun.

"Leo, I played poker with four men—"

"The new man."

"Pardo?"

"That's him."

"What happened to him?"

"He's dead drunk," Vincey said. "I need help carrying him to his room."

"Isn't there anybody else you can ask?"

"Nope," the man said. "Besides, he's your friend, ain't he?"

"No, he's not," Clint said. "I only met him today."

"Well, he was tellin' everybody he was your friend," Vincey said.

"He was?"

"Sure thing."

"Did he tell people my name?"

Vincey looked both ways in the hall before answering. "Not really."

"What do you mean, not really?"

"Can you help me?"

"He's not going anywhere, is he, Leo?" Clint asked.

"Uh, no."

"Then tell me what you meant by 'not really'?"

"Well . . . he told me, but he didn't tell nobody else."

"Are you sure?"

"I'm sure."

"Then, Leo, I guess the next question is . . . who did you tell?"

Vincey looked down at his feet.

"That many people, huh?"

"Well . . . you are a celebrity."

"No, I'm—oh, what's the use? Let me get my pants and I'll give you a hand."

"Thanks, Mr. Ad—uh, thanks."

Clint closed the door on the man and pulled on his trousers. It was clear he was going to have to leave Chester tomorrow. Duke was just going to have to be sound enough to carry him.

NINETEEN

"Kyle's gonna be mad," Evan said.

"About what?" John-Boy asked.

"That we camped instead of riding into town."

"Is he gonna be mad?" John-Boy asked Amanda.

"I don't know, John-Boy," she said, "and I don't care. All I know is I wasn't about to ride into Chester in the dark, not knowing who's there."

"Who's gonna be there?" John-Boy asked.

"Maybe the Gunsmith."

"The guy that killed Linc?"

"That's right."

"Well, ain't we supposed to find him?" John-Boy asked.

"We sure are," Evan said, "and Kyle's gonna be—"

"Evan, shut up about Kyle," Amanda said. "Kyle's not here."

She took the coffeepot off the fire and poured herself another cup. It was good because she had made it herself.

None of her male cousins, or her brothers, could make a cup of coffee worth a damn.

"Amanda?" John-Boy said.

"What?"

"Can I ask you somethin'?"

"Go ahead."

"How come you ain't a-scared of Kyle?"

"Kyle's my brother," Amanda said.

"So? He's my brother, too, and I'm a-scared of him."

"I know how to handle him."

"Really?"

"Yeah."

"Could you teach me?"

"No."

"Why not?"

"Because you're not a woman."

"Well . . . how come you was never a-scared of Linc? He really scared me."

"Well, not me."

"How come?"

"Because he was stupid," she said. "Maybe not as stupid as Hank, and he sure wasn't as stupid as Pete, but he was stupid."

"And you could handle him?"

"Yeah, I could."

"Because you're a girl?"

"Yeah."

"Well," John-Boy said, frowning, "I don't wanna be no girl, so I guess I'll just have to keep being a-scared of Kyle."

"And stupid."

"Huh?"

"I said you'll have to keep being stupid, too," Evan said.

"I may be stupid, but I ain't no more stupid than you," John-Boy said belligerently.

"I ain't stupid, John-Boy," Evan said, "you are."

John-Boy looked at Amanda for confirmation of this.

"Ain't he too stupid, Amanda?"

"Yes, he is, John-Boy."

"Hey—" Evan said.

"You're stupid, Evan," she said, cutting him off, "and dangerous."

Evan frowned. Was being called dangerous bad?

"Whataya mean?"

"I mean you're stupid and you don't know it," she said. "That makes you dangerous."

Evan sat quietly for a few minutes, then he decided he'd been insulted.

"Amanda, I ought to thump you one."

"No, you ain't gonna thump her," John-Boy said.

"Why not?"

"Because she's a girl," John-Boy said. "You cain't hit no girl, ain't that right, Amanda?"

"That's right, baby brother," she said.

" 'Sides," John-Boy said to Evan, "I wouldn't let you hit her."

Amanda reached out and patted John-Boy's shoulder.

"Thank you, baby."

"Baby," Evan said in disgust. "You know what, John-Boy, maybe I oughta just thump you, then."

"Come ahead—"

"That's enough," Amanda said. "Nobody's thumping nobody. Evan, you take the first watch. John-Boy, you take the second."

"And you takin' the third?" Evan demanded.

"No," she said, stretching out on her blanket, "there ain't gonna be a third."

"Why not?"

"Because one of us has to get some sleep," she said. "One of us has to be alert tomorrow."

"And that's gonna be you?" Evan asked.

"That's right."

"Why you?"

"Because I just set the watches, didn't I?" she asked. "You didn't think of it, did you?"

"That ain't no reason—"

"Next time you set the watches and I'll stand one,"

she said. "Now shut up so I can go to sleep."

She rolled away from him and closed her eyes.

"Stupid," she heard Evan said.

"Dumb ass," John-Boy muttered back.

"Shit."

"Booger . . ."

TWENTY

Clint and Leo picked Pardo up from the table he was slumped over and carried him up to his room, which was in the front of the building. They struggled up the stairs with his deadweight and then dragged him down the hall.

"Are you sure he's alive?" Clint asked.

At that point Pardo suddenly snorted.

"He's alive," Vincey said.

They got him into his room and dropped him on the bed, fully dressed.

"Should we take off his clothes?" Vincey asked.

"I'm not taking off his clothes."

"Well, maybe his boots?"

"Okay," Clint said, "I'll take off his boots, but that's it."

"I gotta go down and lock up."

As the man started for the door, Clint said, "Leo?"

"Yeah?"

"Just how many people did you tell who I was?"

"Well . . ." Vincey looked sheepish.

"Everybody?" Clint asked.

"Naw, not everybody," Vincey said, "just, uh, everybody I served a drink to."

"Great," Clint said, "just great. I'll probably have to

sleep with one eye open the rest of the night.''

"I'm really sorry, Mr. Adams," Vincey said, "but you're the most famous person I ever had in my place."

"Yeah . . ."

"Are you, uh, gonna be leavin' now?"

"Yes."

"Tomorrow?"

"As soon as I wake up."

"Because I opened my big mouth?"

"Well . . . I guess it's really because he opened his big mouth," Clint said, indicating the snoring Pardo.

"I'm real sorry you're leavin', but it was a real pleasure havin' you in my place."

"Yeah," Clint said, "thanks . . . I think."

Vincey left and Clint pulled Pardo's boots off and set them on the floor next to the bed. Then he unbuckled the man's gun belt so he wouldn't shoot himself during the night. He hung it on the bedpost, then turned to leave. As he did so he had a clear look out the window, and since there were no tall buildings across the street all he saw was the black night—and something else.

He walked to the window and peered out intently. Was that a light? The flickering light of a campfire? Why would someone camp so close to town? Or did they not know that there was a town nearby?

Well, Chester wasn't much of a town, anyway. He would have bypassed it himself if Duke hadn't come up lame.

He would have liked to have given Duke a few more days' rest, but he was taking the appearance of Pardo— and the flapping of his big mouth, as well as Vincey's—as a sign that he should be on his way. He just wouldn't push Duke very hard for a few days, that's all.

Pardo mumbled in his sleep and rolled over on his side. Clint turned and walked from the window to the door of the room. He stepped out into the hall and pulled the door closed behind him, then walked to his own room, which was off the alley next to the hotel.

He pulled off his own boots again, and then his trousers, and hung his own gun belt on the bedpost. He still had time to get plenty of rest, and then an early start.

He slid between the sheets and thought back to the last time he'd been in bed with Grace Whitney. Her skin had been so pale and warm, her breasts almost plump as she spread them over his chest, lying on top of him. Suddenly, he was getting hard and he shook his head to dispel the image. No point in getting himself all dressed up with no place to go.

He needed a woman soon, though. He wondered, if there had been a whorehouse in Chester, if he would have broken his lifelong rule about not paying for sex.

He rolled over, put out the lamp, and tried not to think about sex at all.

TWENTY-ONE

Clint woke early the next morning, and he was glad to see that his instincts were still working. He checked the time and saw that it was not yet eight a.m. He could get some breakfast, pick up a few supplies when the general store opened at nine, and then be on his way.

He dressed, packed his saddlebags and bedroll, and carried them downstairs with him. This early the saloon was more of a restaurant, the only one in town, actually. Leo Vincey became a cook instead of a bartender. When Clint came down there were several men already having breakfast. He didn't see Pardo anywhere.

It was clear in the way they looked at him that each of these men—two sitting together and one alone—now knew who he was. He walked to a table in the corner and Vincey came over with a pot of coffee for him.

"The usual, Mr. Adams?"

"Sure, Leo, why not?"

"Comin' up."

Vincey was a little more solicitous to him now that he knew who he was. That was another indicator that it was time to leave—that and the way people watched him while he ate. Several men came in and replaced the ones who had been there when he came down, and they also watched him, maybe to see if he ate differently than they did.

He finished his breakfast and turned down a second pot of coffee.

"Got to be on my way, Leo."

Vincey leaned in and whispered, "I'm real sorry about what happened, Mr. Adams."

Why was he whispering now? The whole town knew who he was.

"That's okay, Leo," Clint said.

"You want I should tell your friend anything for you?" Vincey asked.

"For the last time, Leo," Clint said, "Pardo is not my friend. I just met him yesterday."

"Oh, that's right."

Clint shook his head.

"Just tell him I said good-bye, okay?"

"Sure thing."

Clint walked to the door without looking at anyone, although for a moment he entertained the thought of simply turning and bowing to everyone in the room.

He stopped at the general store for a few supplies—some coffee, canned peaches, and a side of bacon—and then went to the livery. He checked Duke over carefully, and there was no hint of a limp.

"I would have liked to have given you a few more days, big boy, but it's time to go. You up to it?"

Duke gave him a baleful look, then turned his head away.

"Dumb question," Clint said. "You're always up to it, aren't you?"

Duke's big head bounced up and down, as if he were nodding in answer to the question.

"Sometimes," Clint said, saddling him, "I think you're the smartest one of the two of us, you know that?"

Again, the nod.

"Wise guy."

• • •

He walked the big gelding outside and then around in a circle a few times before mounting up. Then he rode him around a bit.

"Well, you seem okay," Clint said, patting the big horse's powerful neck. "What do you say we both stay on the lookout for chuckholes, huh?"

Duke didn't nod this time, which was just as well. Sometimes Clint thought the horse knew exactly what he was saying, but then again, he was just a horse, right?

Right, he thought, Duke was just a horse.

"Let's get going, big fella," Clint said, knowing that if Duke was just another horse, he wouldn't spend as much time talking to him, would he?

That would be crazy.

TWENTY-TWO

"You stupid shit!" Evan shouted at his sleeping brother, John-Boy. "You're supposed to be on watch!"

He woke John-Boy with a well-placed kick, and the younger Jensen came bounding up from his seated position in front of the fire.

"I shoulda just tossed you in the fire and woke you up that way."

"Wha—what—"

"What's goin' on?" Amanda demanded, coming awake, as well.

"Instead of staying on watch and waking us up, your little 'baby' brother fell asleep sitting by the fire." Evan looked at John-Boy again. "Shoulda left you alone and let you fall face first into it. *That* woulda woke you up, huh?"

"That woulda been mean," John-Boy said.

"What time is it?" Amanda asked irritably.

"It's late," Evan said. "Must be close to ten."

"Shit!"

John-Boy responded more to Amanda's anger than to Evan's tirade.

"I'm sorry, Amanda," he said. "I was real sleepy."

"John-Boy . . ." she started, and then stopped.

"What?"

"Never mind," she said. "Let's break camp and get movin'."

"What about breakfast?" John-Boy wailed.

"We don't have time for breakfast," Evan said, "thanks to you."

"We'll get somethin' in town," Amanda said. "Don't argue, damn it, let's just *move*!"

TWENTY-THREE

Leo Vincey knew these people were trouble as soon as they walked in—he just didn't know how much.

Pardo had come downstairs an hour after Clint left and was just finishing up his breakfast when Amanda, John-Boy, and Evan Jensen walked into the saloon.

"Can I get a drink?" John-Boy asked.

Vincey didn't know if the simple-looking big one was talking to him or one of his companions.

"We're servin' breakfast," he said aloud, "not liquor."

"It's too early for a drink, John-Boy," Amanda said, "but we'll eat." She looked at Vincey and said it again. "We'll eat."

"Take a seat, then," Vincey said. "I got eggs and potatoes and biscuits."

"Bring it on," Evan said, "and coffee."

"Comin' up."

They took a table and Amanda looked around. There were a few men in the place, all sitting alone and eating.

When Vincey came with the coffee she asked, "We're lookin' for a friend of ours."

"Oh? Who's that?"

"Name's Clint Adams," she said. "Maybe you know him as the Gunsmith."

85

''The Gunsmith,'' Vincey said, feigning surprise. ''I know that name. What would he be doin' here?''

''Maybe just passin' through, same as we are,'' she said.

''Not so's I'd remember,'' Vincey said. ''I'll get you your breakfast.''

He left. Amanda poured herself a cup of coffee and left her brothers to pour their own. John-Boy slopped some on the table, as usual.

''Clumsy,'' Evan said.

''It were an accident,'' John-Boy said.

''So were you.''

''I was not.''

''Shut up, both of you.''

''Excuse me?''

Amanda looked up and saw the dark-haired, good-looking cuss from the corner standing there, looking down at her.

''Yeah?''

''I heard you were looking for a friend,'' he said.

''We don't need no new friends,'' she said.

''No, I mean we have a friend in common.''

''In *where*?'' John-Boy asked.

The man continued to look at Amanda.

''We're both friends with Clint Adams.''

''Is that a fact?''

''It sure is.''

''Well, where is he, then?''

''He was here until this morning. He left a little more than an hour ago.''

''You mean the bartender lied to us?'' Evan asked.

''I don't know what he was thinkin','' Pardo said, ''but Clint was here, all right.''

''But not no more?''

''No, ma'am.''

Amanda realized that this fella was looking her up and

down real good. She had some trail dust on her, but she knew she attracted men.

"Why don't you set a spell, mister? Have some coffee."

"Don't mind if I do."

Pardo sat.

"Hey, barkeep! We need another coffee cup here."

Vincey came out with another cup lopped around his finger, while carrying their breakfasts.

He spread it all out on the table and then asked, "Anything else?"

"Yeah," Amanda said, and looked at Evan. "He lied to us, Evan."

"Can I shoot him, Amanda?"

"Wha—" Vincey said.

"Hey—" Pardo said.

"Shoot him, Evan," Amanda said.

Evan smiled, drew his gun, and shot Vincey in the chest. The man staggered back, slammed against the bar, and fell to the floor.

"Jesus," somebody said, but nobody moved.

"Eat up," she told her brothers, "we're gonna be leavin' soon."

"How soon?" Evan asked.

"Soon as this fella tells us where Clint Adams is."

Pardo was still staring at them in shock. He didn't dare look behind him at Vincey.

"Just sit tight for a minute, handsome," Amanda said. "You got a room?"

"Uh, yeah—"

"I'm gonna have a little somethin' to eat, and then we're goin' to your room."

"We are?"

"Sure."

Pardo stared at the woman. There was no way he could call her pretty. Under the dirt, though, she probably wasn't bad. Her clothes were loose, several sizes too big, but he could see she had breasts and hips.

"It's been a while since I had me a man," she said, chewing her food, then added, "I mean, somebody who wasn't part of my family."

"What?" Pardo asked.

"That won't bother you none, will it, honey?"

Somehow, Pardo knew that "no" was the right answer.

TWENTY-FOUR

Clint had taken a roundabout way out of Chester, still testing Duke's leg. He didn't want to go far and then have him pull up lame again. When he was satisfied that this was not going to happen he headed due south.

Before long he came to the campfire he'd seen from the hotel window last night. He got down and examined the ground. It looked like three riders riding shod horses—probably no pack animals.

He put his hand over the ashes of the fire and found them warm. They'd left not too long ago, heading for Chester. Why, he wondered, would anyone go there if they didn't have to?

Maybe they were looking for someone.

Like him?

He kicked the ashes so they'd spread and cool, and then he mounted Duke. If the Jensens were on his trail, let them find him. Sure, he could have ridden back to Chester, seen if it was them, and got it over with, but he flat out didn't want to. If they were going to hunt him down and force him to kill them, let them work at it for a while.

"Come on," he said to Duke, "fuck 'em."

TWENTY-FIVE

In spite of the fact that he was scared, Pardo had an erection.

"Whooeee," Amanda said, "that's mighty pretty."

She was standing next to the bed, naked. She had full breasts and hips, well developed arms and legs. She stood five four, and except for the fact that she hadn't taken real good care of her teeth—some were missing, some were just black—she didn't look too bad.

Pardo loved women, and Amanda had real nice breasts with big, brown nipples, and while she didn't smell too clean, he could smell her readiness there between her legs.

Jesus, he thought, I'm a real hound if this bitch in heat can get me hard.

"Just lie there, handsome," Amanda said, "I'm gonna do all the work."

She slid the fingers of one hand around his penis and began to stroke it.

"Mmm-mm," she said, "ain't that the prettiest tally-wacker I ever did see? Much better than any of my brothers'."

The thought of her being with any of her brothers made him feel sick, but what she was doing to his pecker was making him feel a lot better.

"Now, I know I ain't got the prettiest mouth, and my teeth are bad," she said to him, "but you tell me if this don't feel good."

And with that she bent over and took him in her mouth and started sucking on him to beat the band.

"Oh, yeah," he said, lifting his hips some, "that feels . . . good . . ."

She let his pecker slide loose from her mouth for a moment and said, "You kin fiddle with me some while I'm tasting you, handsome."

She went back to sucking and he slid his hand over her breasts, tweaking her nipples, then around behind her to stroke her butt, and then finally between her legs where he found her wet and ready.

"Oh, God," she said when he touched her there, "what the—hey, what—"

"Hasn't anybody ever touched you there?" he asked.

"Well, no . . . I mean, I was thinking you'd touch my teats and all, but . . . oh, what's *that*?"

"That's where all your pleasure comes from, sweetie," he said, stroking her little nub until it stood up straight.

"Oh my God," she said, "my legs is gone—I got to lie down—"

She got in bed with him, her skin hot to the touch.

"I shoulda washed up, I know that, but—"

"We're past that now, honey," Pardo said, slipping one finger fully inside of her.

"Oh, honey, aint we!" she cried.

Downstairs John-Boy and Evan sat waiting. The bartender, Vincey, was still lying on the floor in front of the bar. The other diners had very carefully left, ignored by the two Jensen brothers.

Suddenly, there was a loud cry, almost a squeal, from upstairs.

"What's she doin' up there?" John-Boy asked.

"Whataya think, dummy?"

John-Boy looked surprised.

"She's doin' *that* with that stranger?"

"You bet."

"But why?"

"John-Boy," Evan said, "you got a lot to learn about women, don't you?"

"Like what?" John-Boy asked curiously.

"Like they got a itch only a man can scratch."

"They do?"

"You ever scratched a woman's itch, John-Boy? I'll bet you ain't."

"I scratched Maw's back once, when she couldn't reach it."

Evan laughed.

"That ain't the kind of itch I'm talkin' about," he said. "I'm talking about the one they got between their legs."

"Oh," John-Boy said, blushing and looking away.

"Ain't you ever been with even a whore?"

"No," he mumbled.

Suddenly, Evan's attitude changed. He became solicitous of his younger brother.

"Well, you know what? When we're done with this, ol' Evan's gonna take you to one."

"Really?"

"We're gonna get your wick wet, boy," Evan said, laughing, and John-Boy laughed with him—until there was another squeal from upstairs, and then they both stopped and listened.

"Maybe he's hurtin' her," John-Boy said, looking concerned.

Evan laughed and said, "Take my advice, boy. He ain't hurtin' her."

"So what are we gonna do?"

"We're just gonna sit here and wait," Evan said. He looked over at the dead bartender. "And get ourselves some drinks."

Evan got up and went behind the bar.

"What about the law?" John-Boy asked.

"I think if there was any law in this town," Evan said, "they would have been here by now, don't you?"

TWENTY-SIX

"Oh, God," Amanda said. She was sitting astride Pardo now, his penis buried to the hilt inside of her. His hands were on her breasts, squeezing them and tweaking her nipples.

"Ooh, yeah, darlin'," Amanda said. "Mmm-hmmm, you're all the way up in me, ain'tcha?"

"You bet I am!"

"Oooh, you doin' it to me now, ain'tcha?"

Pardo grunted his reply. As she rode up and down on him, he lifted his hips to meet her, and she was heavier than she looked—although he should have known that from her breasts and butt.

Amanda got quiet then as she started lifting up and coming down on him harder and harder—quiet in that she stopped talking and was just grunting and squealing now.

Pardo reached one hand down between them and touched her where they were joined, and that pushed her over the edge. She howled loudly, almost causing his ears to ring, and then he let go and exploded inside of her, which made her eyes bug out in a comical way. She pulled her lips back from her teeth, which wasn't exactly a pretty sight. Now that Pardo was done with her, he wanted to get her off of him and out of his room as soon as he could. With his passion sated, she wasn't the least bit appealing anymore. At the moment she smelled sweaty and dirty, and he wrinkled his nose in response.

"Whoa," she said, looking down at him.

"Yeah," he said. "I, uh, gotta get up."

"Relax, honey," she said, putting both hands on his chest and pushing him down. "We still got to talk about the Gunsmith."

"Well," Pardo said sheepishly, "to tell you the truth, we ain't really friends."

"You ain't?"

"No," Pardo said. "In fact, we only just met yesterday."

"Is that a fact?"

"Yeah, it is."

She wiggled her hips, moving him around inside of her. He was semi-hard, but softening fast.

"So, you wouldn't know where he went, would you?"

"No," he said, "not at all."

"Hmm," she said, arching her back and reaching behind her. The move made her breasts stand out, and she did have nice nipples. Maybe just one more time, he thought, and started to get hard again.

"Oooh," she said, "something's happening inside of me."

"It sure is."

She was still reaching behind her, like she was grabbing for something.

"So then," she said, "when you said you was friends with him, you lied to us."

"I guess I, uh—" he started to reply, but then he suddenly remembered what had happened to Vincey when he was caught lying to them.

"Hey, wait—" he said, but it was too late.

Reaching behind her she finally got hold of her gun and brought it around to point it at his face.

"I hate liars," she said, and pulled the trigger.

Immediately blood spread out on the pillow beneath his head, because he had lifted his head just before the shot. That didn't concern Amanda, though. Rather, she looked down between her legs, where he had slipped out, and said, "Oh, you went all soft on me."

At the sound of the shot John-Boy sat up and started to get out of his chair, but Evan stopped him.

"She'll be down directly."

"But—"

"That was her gun."

"You sure?"

"Just sit."

John-Boy looked dubious, but settled back.

Moments later they heard a door open upstairs, and then Amanda came down the stairs, strapping on her gun. As she came closer they could smell her, a sweaty smell. Evan smirked, because he recognized the smell.

"Have a good time?" he asked.

"Yeah, I did," she said. She didn't bother pulling up a chair to sit.

"Is he dead?" John-Boy asked.

"Yeah," she said, "he's dead."

"Why?"

"Maybe he wasn't so good in bed," Evan said, snickering.

"Because he lied to us," she said.

"I hate liars," Evan said, his face darkening. He looked over at the dead bartender once more, wishing he could shoot him again.

"About what?" John-Boy asked.

"He didn't know Clint Adams. He just met him yesterday."

"So he don't know where he went, huh?" Evan asked.

"No," Amanda said.

"What do we do now?" John-Boy asked.

"We head south," Evan said. He looked at Amanda for confirmation.

She nodded and said, "Jacksboro."

TWENTY-SEVEN

Clint had no way of knowing if the people from the campsite were members of the Jensen family or not—but even if they were, he wasn't about to run. He kept Duke to a steady but easy pace, and knew he wouldn't make Jacksboro by dark. Instead, he camped about two hours' ride from it, figuring to ride in come morning and get some more supplies. Also, if they had a telegraph—and they probably would—he figured to send a message to his friend Rick Hartman in Labyrinth, to see what he knew about Kyle Jensen and his family.

He unsaddled Duke and checked the horse's leg thoroughly even before building a fire. When that was done he opened a can of peaches and ate it, washing it down with strong trail coffee.

By the light of the fire he spent time checking his weapons, telling himself that he did this every so often anyway, and it had nothing to do with the Jensens.

He settled back after that and just stared at the night sky. He'd sleep lightly tonight, just in case, but then again he always slept lightly when he was camped. It was just a built-in survival mechanism that kicked in by itself. He'd sleep light enough for Duke to wake him if the big horse sensed anyone coming—or anything. He remembered a time when Duke woke him just before a bear came raging into camp. It had been wounded by some hunters and was mad with pain. He'd had to shoot it several times before he finally put it down.

Between the two of them they managed to keep each other alive. Clint started to feel some guilt over Duke's recent injury. He should have seen that chuckhole. He would have, a few years ago. Maybe he was just getting old—too old for the trail.

No, that wasn't it. He was still too young to settle down in some town. What would he do, anyway?

Clint spread his blanket and took his gun out of his holster. He'd hold it in his hand while he slept. He'd done that before, and wouldn't recommend it to anyone with less experience than he. He felt certain that he'd never discharge it accidently and shoot himself in the foot, or worse.

He stoked the fire some to make sure it wouldn't go out, then checked the coffeepot to make sure there was some left. When he woke he'd want a cup, and it didn't matter to him how long it sat on the fire.

Settling down to sleep, he laid his hat aside, folded his arms across his chest, and closed his eyes.

"We're camping again?" Evan asked.

"We ain't ridin' at night," Amanda said, "and neither is Adams. The liveryman said his horse was still recovering from a leg injury."

"Yeah," John-Boy said, giggling, "just before you hit him."

Amanda ignored the remark. The liveryman was looking at her funny, like he knew from the way she smelled that she'd been with a man. She didn't want anyone taking liberties with her, so she hit him.

"The point is, Adams ain't gonna push his horse. And there's another thing."

"What's that?" Evan asked.

"He's headed for Jacksboro," Amanda said.

"Like us," John-Boy said.

"And like Kyle and the others," Amanda said.

"Oh, yeah," Evan said. "So we may all be there."

"That's right," Amanda said.

"And Adams will be in big trouble," John-Boy said.

"Right again. I'm gonna make coffee. You boys bed down the horses."

"Sure thing, Amanda," John-Boy said.

She was surprised when Evan didn't argue. She was also surprised that he didn't seem to be picking on John-Boy so much anymore—not since they'd left Chester, anyway.

John-Boy and Evan were almost acting like—well, brothers.

TWENTY-EIGHT

The wind woke Clint.

He sat up straight and felt the wind and the sand it was whipping up strike his face. It felt like insects with tiny little stingers.

Immediately he remembered what the old man in Chester had said, that a wind was coming. This must have been what he meant. No rain, just wind, and a pretty damned strong one, at that.

Duke was sniffing the air and shuffling around. Clint looked at the sky, but it was partially obscured by the wind. He thought it was early morning, but he couldn't be sure.

He got up and quickly gathered his things. He noticed that the wind had not only blown out the fire, but it had scattered the ashes, as well.

He saddled Duke, talking to him the whole while to keep him calm.

"We're going to have to find some shelter, boy," he said, tying his bedroll on, "before this wind gets any worse."

They were also going to have to find something before the visibility got any worse.

He swung into the saddle, grabbed up the reins—and stopped.

"Shit," he said. "Which way did we come, and which way were we going?"

The wind and the sand made it difficult to figure out directions. Finally, he just decided to pick one and get moving.

Next time some old man told him he could smell the wind coming, he was going to believe him.

The wind also woke the Jensens—Amanda, John-Boy, and Evan.

"What's happening?" John-Boy asked.

"Some kind of storm," Amanda said. "We're gonna have to find shelter."

"I can't hardly see," Evan said, as they all went to saddle their horses, who were skittish.

"Don't let your horse go, or it'll run," she shouted above the sound of the wind.

They saddled their horses and hung on tight to them while stowing their gear. Then they mounted up.

"Which way?" Evan asked.

"There," Amanda said, pointing.

She didn't know which way she was pointing, but she didn't want her brothers knowing that. Whichever way they went they were going to have to forget about Jacksboro for now. They just needed to find a place to wait out this wind. Luckily, she thought, Clint Adams was in the same position.

TWENTY-NINE

The wind was getting worse. The sand was starting to feel like needles in their skin. They had their bandannas covering their faces, but they were starting to be able to feel the sting through their clothes.

"If we don't find somethin' soon," Amanda called out, "and this wind gets any worse, we might have to gut the horses and use them for shelter."

"I ain't guttin' ol' Bucky," John-Boy called back.

"How many times I gotta tell you," Evan told him, "don't never name some animal you might someday have to eat!"

"I ain't eatin' him, neither!"

Clint knew that if he were riding a lesser animal than Duke, just "some horse," he'd be thinking about using the animal for shelter right about now.

But not Duke.

Visibility was almost completely gone, partly because he had to keep his eyes squinted against the wind and sand. With his bandanna pulled up over his mouth and his hat pulled down over his eyes, he was feeling the sting of the sand and wind on his body, and Duke was showing signs of discomfort.

Suddenly, there was a structure in front of him, as if it appeared out of nowhere. He could see the shape and size of it, and figured it was a barn. He headed for it.

Up close he could see that it was, indeed, a barn. He rode up to the doors and without dismounting reached out and tried them. One of the doors swung open, and with a feeling of relief he guided Duke inside.

The wind pounded on the sides of the barn, but inside it was calm. Clint dismounted and pulled his bandanna away from his face. He rubbed his hands over his face, trying to dislodge the sand, and then took a look around. There were several other horses in the barn, some of them looking as if they had recently been ridden. Apparently there were some others who had found this sanctuary, as well . . . but where were they?

As he started to unsaddle Duke he heard the barn door open behind him. He turned and saw a man enter. He was a tall man in his fifties with sandy, thinning hair that came to a widow's peak. He wore a work shirt, jeans and suspenders, and had the look of a rancher.

"Hello, friend."

"Hello," Clint said. "I hope you don't mind. The wind—"

"I know," the man said, "the wind brought you here. I believe the Lord guided you here for shelter, and I shall provide it, just as I have provided for others."

Clint looked over at the other horses.

"Three others are here?"

"Why, yes," the man said, "three people did ride up just a little while before you did."

"Where are we, if you don't mind my asking?"

"Well, you're still in Texas, friend. Where were you headed?"

"Jacksboro."

"Then you came a long way the other way. You traveled west, which puts you about a half day's ride from

Jacksboro by now. But no matter. You are welcome to sit out the storm here for as long as it takes. We'll be cramped, but I will make room for all.''

"Do you have a family?" Clint asked, rubbing Duke down as they talked.

"I have a wife, and a daughter, but we have plenty of food to feed all of us for one night, certainly."

"I'm very grateful," Clint said. "If I had seen the house before the barn I would have asked permission."

"No need to apologize. If you're ready, I'll take you to the house. It would be very easy for you to get lost between here and there."

"I'll just feed my horse a little something, if you don't mind."

"Oats or hay," the man said, "take your choice, friend."

Clint gave Duke some oats, and then turned to face the man.

"My name is Silas," the man said, "and you are most welcome."

Clint hesitated, almost gave his name, and then said, "Thank you."

"No need to give me your name, if you've no mind to," Silas said.

Clint didn't answer. He couldn't explain it, he just had the feeling he should hang on to his name for a while.

He followed Silas to the door, and the man reached out a hand to him.

"Clasp my hand, friend, and I'll lead you to the promised land—my house, that is," Silas said, and laughed at his own joke.

THIRTY

Silas had strung a rope from the house to the barn, and he and Clint followed it back to the house.

When Clint entered the house with Silas, the tension in the air was palpable. There were three people there with an attractive older woman and a pretty, younger woman. The older woman was obviously Silas's wife and was in her fifties as he was. The younger woman was his daughter, and she was in her twenties.

The other three were two men and a woman. Clint had no way of knowing if these were Jensen family members, but there was obviously a family resemblance between the two men. The woman, though dirty, was well built and would have been attractive if she cleaned up and took care of her teeth.

"Rachel," Silas said to his wife, "we have another guest."

"Esther," the woman said to her daughter, "set another place at the table."

The house had obviously been built with loving care, probably by Silas. It also appeared to have been done in two sections, the second probably added to the first after some years. There was a hallway in the rear that obviously led to other rooms.

The other three strangers were sitting comfortably in the living room until Clint entered. Now the two men were leaning forward in their chairs. The woman, however, still appeared calm, and the two men seemed to be looking to her for a sign.

"These three people," Silas said, indicating the other three strangers, "were also blown here by the wind. Like you, they also have their reasons for not giving their names. And as with you, we will feed and shelter them, anyway."

"You're very kind," Clint said, "you and your family."

"That's what we said," the woman chimed in. "You don't find too many people these days willing to take in strangers."

"On a night like this," Silas said, "I would like to think that anyone would extend the same kindnesses we are."

"You can think that all you like, mister," one of the men said, "but it ain't true."

Clint Adams and the three Jensens stared at each other while Silas, his wife, and daughter went about setting the table for dinner.

Amanda Jensen studied Clint critically, wondering if he was, indeed, Clint Adams. Was this what a legend looked like? If it was, he was older than she thought and, probably because of the storm, he was just as dirty.

Clint, in turn, studied the three Jensens. Just because the two men were apparently brothers did not mean they were "Jensen" brothers.

Clint hoped that if these were Jensens they wouldn't try anything while they were all guests of Silas and his family. It seemed to Clint that Silas and his wife and daughter were oblivious to any possibility of danger in their house.

In looking around Clint surmised that Silas and his family were very religious. There were crucifixes on more than one wall and, of course, just from the way the man spoke, he seemed to be filled with the milk of human kindness.

Clint hoped that he and Silas's other three guests would do nothing to disrupt this.

When they were all seated for dinner Clint and the three Jensens—still having no confirmation of each other's identity—gave their full attention to the food on the table—after, of course, they had all washed up at their host's behest.

"Of course," he said, "you'll be wanting to wash off that devil's sand from your bodies."

Well, they washed it from their hands and faces, which seemed to please everyone well enough.

With the dirt and sand washed from the woman's face, Clint was able to make out Amanda Jensen's features. He still saw no resemblance to the men, but they could have taken after one side of the family, while she took after another. Still, with her face clean she looked younger and more attractive—and might have been pretty if she weren't wearing such a stern look all the time.

It was Silas's daughter, however, who was the true beauty in the house. Sitting right across from her, Clint could see that she was no more than twenty-two or-three, fresh-faced, slender, delicately put together. Not his type— too young and slender—but certainly a beautiful girl.

Which, he saw, had not escaped the notice of the other two men, each of whom kept throwing glances her way during dinner. The older man's looks were bold, while the younger man seemed embarrassed by his interest.

The dinner was a beef stew as good or better than any Clint had ever tasted. Everyone at the table seemed to agree, for in the end there was none left.

"Well," Silas said over coffee and peach pie, "perhaps you good people can tell us where you were headed when the storm drove you our way. This fellow," he said, indicating Clint, "says he was on his way to Jacksboro."

"I was going in that direction," Clint said. "It was not my ultimate destination."

"Us, too," Amanda said. "I mean, we was headin' in that direction."

"I see," Silas said. "Well, I'm afraid the storm has added a half day to your ride—presuming, of course, that it lets up by morning and allows you all to be on your way."

"We're not from Texas," Amanda said. "How long do these storms usually last?"

"I'm afraid I don't know," Silas said. "You see, I've never seen anything like this."

In that moment they all fell silent and listened to the wind howling outside. It sounded as if it were beating against the walls and the roof, trying to tear the house down.

"Can this house stand up to that wind?" Evan asked.

"The house is very well built," Silas said. "I built it myself, but . . . as I said, I have never seen this kind of wind before. I suppose we'll just have to wait and see."

They all exchanged glances and Silas's wife, Rachel, asked, "Would anyone like more coffee?"

Later Silas spoke of the sleeping arrangements.

"I'm afraid you gentlemen will have to make do out here," he said, indicating the living room area of the house. "There is plenty of floor space."

"You can sleep in my room . . ." Esther told Amanda.

"Amanda," she replied, "my name is Amanda."

"Amanda," Esther said, "that's a pretty name."

Clint noticed that Amanda seemed to be thrown off balance by the compliment.

"Come on," Esther said, "I think I have something you can wear to go to sleep."

Before Amanda could protest, Esther had grabbed her hand and pulled her down the hall to her room, closing the door after them.

"My wife will get blankets for the three of you," Silas said, "and then we'll say good night."

THIRTY-ONE

Clint and the two men whose names he still didn't know eyed each other as they held their blankets. They were each wondering where the best place to bed down would be.

Finally, Clint said, "I think I'll bed down over here on the other side of the door." That way no one would be able to enter or leave without waking him.

"We'll bed down over here," Evan said, indicating a space on the other side of the house from Clint.

"Yeah," John-Boy said, "over here."

"Shut up, John-Boy," Evan said. "Don't repeat what I say."

"Okay, Evan."

"And don't say my name!"

"You said mine!"

"Shut up and put down your blanket."

The two men proceeded to lay out their blankets while muttering either to themselves or to each other, Clint couldn't tell which.

Clint laid his blanket out, then lifted his head and listened.

"What is it?" Evan asked, noticing from across the room.

"I thought I heard the horses," Clint said. "I think I'm going to go check on the animals in the barn."

"That old man said you could get lost between here and the barn."

"I think I can find the way," Clint said. "Silas left a rope trail. I'll just check on all the animals, yours included."

"Well," Evan said, "suit yourself."

Clint tied his bandanna around his face and pulled his hat down low over his eyes, then opened the door and stepped out into the storm.

He paused outside to get his bearings, then started toward the barn, using the rope to guide him. He tried to fix in his mind where the house was, just in case the rope broke, or was blown away.

When he reached the barn he hurried inside and pulled the door closed behind him. It was calm inside, and the horses seemed calm, as well. He hadn't really thought he heard a horse. He'd just said that to try to lure the two men out of the house. If they were Jensens, and they thought he was—well, himself—they'd probably follow him out to try to do away with him.

Clint walked over to the stall where Duke was standing easy and touched the animal, just to let him know he was there.

"Easy, boy," he said, patting the animal's neck. "We might have some company, or we might not. Let's wait and see."

While he was waiting he went over to the other horses. There were five. Obviously, two were Silas's, and the other three belonged to the woman and two men. Clint examined all five and was able to pick out the three which had just arrived before him. He could tell by their condition which ones they were.

He checked for brands and found none, and there were no other markings on the animals that would help him identify them or their owners.

He moved away from the animals then and to the door, where he stopped to listen, but all he could hear was the wind.

Maybe he was wrong. Maybe they weren't Jensens, but even if they weren't they were wrong types, he could tell that. If they weren't on the run, they were on the prowl. Even the woman projected that.

He waited about fifteen minutes before he pulled the hat back down over his eyes, the bandanna back up over his mouth, and opened the door to step out. That's when he knew there was trouble.

The rope had gone slack.

THIRTY-TWO

Had the rope blown loose, or had someone untied it from the house? And if they had untied it, were they outside or inside?

What did they expect to happen? That he'd get lost and never find his way back? All he had to do was walk in an ever widening circle until he found the house—and that was only if he didn't feel confident enough to walk in a straight line to it—and he thought he could do that.

So what was going on in the house now?

It had been Evan's idea to untie the rope.

"Why are you doin' that?" John-Boy asked.

"Because it's him."

"Who?"

"The Gunsmith."

Evan closed the door after he'd loosened the rope.

"Now what?" John-Boy asked.

Before Evan could answer Silas entered the room, wearing a sleeping gown.

"I heard the door open. What's happened?"

At that point Evan pulled his gun, and Amanda came walking down the hall with hers, leading Esther ahead of her. She was still wearing her own clothes, even though

117

Esther had tried to give her some cleaner ones.

"Stay here," she said to the young woman. To Evan she said, "I'll get the other woman."

"What's going on?" Silas asked.

"Shut up," Evan said. "You'll find out soon enough."

Amanda came out leading the older woman in her dressing gown. Her long hair was braided for sleeping, and she looked frightened, as did the daughter.

"I heard the door open," Amanda said to her brothers, "and I knew you was doin' something stupid."

"It was Evan's idea," John-Boy said.

"Shut up," Evan said. "It's him, Amanda. I know it."

"Yeah, I feel it, too," Amanda said. "Where did he get to?"

"He said he was goin' out to check the horses," Evan said. "Said he thought he heard somethin', but I didn't hear nothin'. If my horse was actin' up I'd know it."

"And then what did you do?"

"I untied the rope the old man set up from the house to the barn."

"Well," Amanda said, "that'll keep him out there for a while—long enough for us to get ready for him, anyway."

"What is going on?" Silas asked. "Who are you people?"

"We're the people who are gonna shoot you and your family if you don't shut up," Amanda said. "Now sit down at the table."

Esther gave Amanda a withering look and said, "You are a horrible woman."

"You got that right, sweetie," Amanda said. "Now sit down and shut up, like I told you."

Silas and his family sat down. He maintained a stoic silence only after telling the wife and daughter, "It will be all right. The Lord will protect us."

"What are we gonna do now?" John-Boy asked. "Wait for him?"

Amanda ignored his question and looked at Evan.

"I wish you'd asked me before you untied the rope," she said accusingly.

"Why do I need your permission?"

"Okay, smart guy," she said. "What do we do next? Wait for him, or go out and get him?"

"Why would we go out and get him?" he asked. "He's gotta come back here or wander around—"

"What if he just stays in the barn?"

"Why would he do that?"

"Because he's got to do something when he sees that the rope was untied."

"What if he just thinks it blew away in the wind?" Evan asked.

"I don't think there's much chance of that, Evan," she said. "This is the Gunsmith we're dealing with, here. He's gonna play it careful."

"Okay, so then what do you think we should do?"

"You're askin' me?" she said, looking surprised. "A girl?"

"Come on, Amanda," he said.

"I think you and John-Boy should go out there and get him."

"Why us?" Evan asked.

"Who's better with a gun, Evan?" she asked innocently. "You or me?"

Evan frowned. He'd never admit that she was better— especially not in front of Silas and his family.

"Somebody has to stay in here and keep an eye on them," Amanda went on.

"Why do we have to go out and get him?" John-Boy asked. His voice was a whine, like a child's.

"Because he ain't comin' in here, John-Boy."

"But we got them."

"He don't care about them," she said. "He cares about himself."

"What if we get lost out there?" John-Boy asked.

"You won't," she said. "I'm gonna light all the lamps in the house. You should be able to find it with no problem."

"But it's dark."

"I know it's dark, John-Boy," she said. "That's why lighting the lamps will make it easier to find."

"Come on," Evan said. "Let's get this done."

"You still gonna take me to a whorehouse when this is done, Evan?" John-Boy asked.

"Sure," Evan said. But he looked at Silas's wife and daughter and added, "But why waste money? You can have your pick right here."

"Really?" John-Boy said. He looked at the two women. "I want the young one."

"That figures," Evan said. "Okay, I'll take the old one. She ain't so bad."

"And Amanda can have the old man," John-Boy said, smiling.

"Why don't you two shut up and get goin'?" Amanda demanded.

"We're goin', Amanda," Evan said, "but when we get back you ain't tellin' us what to do."

Amanda didn't answer.

After the men left Silas looked at her.

"You're not going to let them . . . touch the women, are you?"

"Why not?" Amanda asked. "Besides, I probably couldn't stop them if I wanted to."

Esther whimpered and moved close to her mother, who put a protective arm around her.

"Silas," she said, "do something."

"You are obviously a lot smarter than they are," Silas said to Amanda. "You can stop them."

"Why would I want to?"

"It would be the . . . decent thing to do."

"Are you a preacher?"

"No," he said, "I just believe in the Lord."

"Well, then," she said, "maybe He can do somethin' to stop them, 'cause I can't."

"And this other man?" Silas asked. "The one you wish to kill. You think he is the Gunsmith?"

"Yes."

"What if he is not? You will have killed an innocent man."

"You think that bothers me, Padre?"

"I told you, I am not—"

"Well, you sound like one, that's for sure."

"Surely, you can't—"

She moved closer to him and stuck her gun in his face.

"I've heard enough out of you."

Esther started to cry.

"And you stop cryin'!" she said. "I can't stand cryin'."

"Haven't you ever cried?" Rachel asked Amanda.

Amanda thought back to the first time any of the men in her family had used her. No, she hadn't cried, even then.

"No," Amanda said, "I ain't never cried."

"I feel sorry for you," Rachel said.

"Well, you better start feelin' sorry for you and yours," Amanda said. "I don't need your sympathy, but your husband and daughter might."

"You aren't going to . . . touch my husband . . ."

"Don't worry, lady," she said. "He's all yours. What would I want with an old man like him?"

"How could you—" Esther said, but Amanda exploded, cutting her off.

"Just shut up now, all of you!" she shouted. "I've had enough."

"So have I, Amanda," Clint said from behind her. "Put the gun down."

THIRTY-THREE

Instead of putting her gun down Amanda pointed it at Esther's head and cocked the hammer. The room became dead silent. Even Esther was too scared to make a sound.

"Amanda, that's not a good idea."

"How'd you get in here?"

"A window."

Clint had trusted his instincts and had made his way directly back to the house. By looking in the front window he had seen what the situation was, and had gone around the back.

"You are Clint Adams, right?" she asked.

"That's right. You're members of the Jensen family?"

"That's right," she said. "Linc and Hank were our cousins."

"So Pete sent for you?"

"That's right."

"Where's he?"

"He's with my brother Kyle and the others."

"Others?"

"Some more brothers, a cousin or two. There ain't no way you can get away from us."

"Well, that remains to be seen," Clint said. "Right now we have to deal with this problem right here."

"The problem here is easy," Amanda said. "You put your gun down or I blow this little lady's head off."

"And what does that solve? I'll kill you if you do that, and then I'll kill your brothers."

"They might kill you."

"Without you to help them? You really think that's likely, Amanda?"

"So what do you suggest?"

"Put down your gun and walk out. You and your brothers can stay in the barn overnight and head out in the morning."

"Just like that?"

"Just like that," Clint said. "Believe it or not, I'm not looking to kill any more members of the Jensen family. What do you say?"

"If I put my gun down you'll kill me, anyway."

"You have my word I won't."

She hesitated and then said, "If you let us go we'll just join up with the others and hunt you down."

"That's a chance I'll have to take," Clint said, "but it'll solve this little problem right here, won't it?"

"It might . . ." she conceded.

Clint would always wonder what would have happened next if the front door hadn't opened, admitting both John-Boy and Evan. Amanda's two brothers took in the scene in an instant and went for their guns.

"No!" Amanda shouted, but she was too late.

There were too many innocent people in the room for Clint to try anything fancy. He had no choice but to shoot, and shoot accurately.

His first shot hit John-Boy in the chest and exploded his heart, killing him instantly. His second shot hit Evan in the sternum, making his eyes bug out as all of the air was driven from his body. He fell on his back and lay there gasping. Clint knew he'd be dead in minutes.

Amanda turned and faced Clint with her gun.

"Don't do it, Amanda," he said. "We can still have a deal."

"You just killed my brothers."

"Evan's not dead, but he will be in minutes. You've got time to say something to him if you drop your gun now."

She hesitated, and Evan's gasping for breath filled the room.

"Speak to your brother," Silas implored her.

She looked down at Evan, then at Clint.

"Oh damn," she said, and dropped her gun.

She hurried to her brother, got on the floor next to him, and pulled his head into her lap.

"You're a damn fool, you know that, Evan?" she asked. "A damned fool."

THIRTY-FOUR

Silas and Clint braved the storm to put the dead bodies outside. Clint kept Amanda's gun, but it didn't appear that she would be a threat for the rest of the night. Even so he made her bed down on the floor in the room with him rather than in any of the other rooms. Esther certainly didn't want the woman who had threatened to blow her head off to share her room.

When morning came Clint stood up and looked out the window. He was amazed that everything was calm and the sun was shining. In the aftermath of the storm there was some debris thrown around, but there didn't seem to be any major damage to the structure of the barn or the house.

Rachel awoke and fixed breakfast for all of them. She and Esther sat across the table from Amanda, who ate in silence and without looking at anyone.

Afterward Rachel packed some supplies for Clint, who thanked her and took Amanda outside with him to talk to Silas.

"What's the nearest town?" Clint asked.

"For you? In the direction you're headed—"

"No," Clint said, "for you, preferably one with a law-man."

127

"That'd be due east of here," Silas said, "Ryanville."

"Go there," Clint said, "tell the sheriff what happened here, so he'll be on the lookout for the rest of the Jensen family."

Silas looked over to where Amanda was standing silently.

"Are they all . . . like that?" he asked.

"I guess so," Clint said.

"And they are after you?"

Clint nodded.

"For killing two of them in Missouri," he told Silas.

"And now two here."

"Yes."

"They did not give you any choice."

"I know," Clint said. "That doesn't make me like it any better."

"Are you truly the Gunsmith?"

"Yes."

"I suspect your reputation is slightly exaggerated," the man said. "You do not seem to me to be a man who is quick to kill."

"Thank you," Clint said, "I'm not."

"What will you do with her?" Silas asked.

"I don't know," Clint said. "I can't leave her here, and I can't just let her go. I'll have to take her with me, even if it's just for a while."

"What shall I do with her . . . her brothers?" Silas asked. "Bury them?"

"No," Clint said. "You have a buckboard?"

"Yes."

"Put them in there and take them to Ryanville with you," Clint said. "That should be enough to convince the sheriff that this is serious."

"All right." Silas held out his hand and Clint took it. "Want to thank you. You saved my family."

"You gave me shelter."

"It was God's will that we come together," Silas said. "May He ride with you."

"Thank you."

Clint moved away from the house to where Amanda was standing, her shoulders slumped.

"Let's go."

They walked to the barn where Clint told her to saddle her horse, and he set about saddling Duke.

"What are you gonna do with me?"

"I haven't decided yet," Clint said, "but I can't leave you here to hurt these people."

"I don't want to hurt them."

"I'm sure."

"I want to hurt you," she said. "If you take me with you, I'll kill you first chance I get."

"You'll try."

"My brother Kyle, and the others, they'll track you down."

"In Jacksboro, right?" he asked. "Well, we're going to bypass Jacksboro. If they want to find me they're going to have to look real hard."

"They will," she said. "They won't stop, don't think they will."

"I don't think that," Clint said. "If they're anything like you, I know they won't."

"They're not like me," she said. "They've got Kyle with them, and he's smart, and good with a gun."

"Yeah, yeah, I know," Clint said. "All you Jensens are quick with a gun, and eager to show it, aren't you?"

"Kyle's different," she said.

"Like Linc was different?"

"Kyle's better than Linc."

Clint told her to mount up, then did so himself. They rode out of the barn. She looked over to where her brothers were lying beside the house like stacked wood, then she looked at Clint.

"That's not my fault," he said. "None of it is. If you had all just left me alone—"

"We'll never leave you alone," she said, "until you're dead."

"I know that," he said, "now."

THIRTY-FIVE

The storm kept Kyle Jensen, Pete Jensen, and the others from reaching Jacksboro until two days after they were supposed to meet with Amanda, Evan, and John-Boy.

Kyle, Vern, Dave, and Pete Jensen rode into Jacksboro hungry and tired. They left their horses at the livery, then went and checked into the hotel, taking three rooms: one for Kyle, one for Pete, and the third room for Vern and Dave.

While at the hotel Kyle checked to see if Amanda had checked in.

"Dave? Vern? Check around town. See if she and the others checked in at another hotel or rooming house."

"We're hungry, Kyle," Dave whined.

"And thirsty," Vern said.

"Do it and meet us at the saloon nearest to this hotel. You do what I tell you, now."

"Oh, all right," Dave said, and he and Vern left the hotel, leaving their gear behind for Kyle and the others to put in their room.

"What if they ain't here, Kyle?" Pete asked.

"They probably got caught in the same storm we did," Kyle said. "If they ain't here they should be gettin' here directly. Let's just clean up, get something to eat and drink, and wait."

When Dave and Vern met Kyle and Pete at the Yellow Dog Saloon they were shaking their heads.

"They ain't anywhere, Kyle," Dave said.

Vern went to the bar and got a beer for him and Dave, and grabbed some hard-boiled eggs for the two of them. Kyle and Pete already had drinks, and they had eaten something at the hotel.

Vern set the beer and eggs down and sat down with his kin.

"What do we do now?" he asked.

"We wait," Kyle said.

"How long?" Pete asked. "The longer we wait, the further away Adams gets."

Kyle looked at Pete.

"You lost your brothers," he said, "I still have mine, and my sister. I ain't leavin' until I know if they're comin' or not."

"And if they don't?" Vern asked, peeling an egg.

"Then we'll probably have even more reason to kill Clint Adams."

"You think they ran into Adams?" Dave asked.

"I think if they don't show up here, they ran into somethin'," Kyle said. "Clint Adams is a better guess than most."

"If he killed Amanda, John-Boy, and Evan," Vern said, "we should hear about it somehow."

"If they're dead," Kyle said, "and they been identified, maybe the family at home got notified. Vern, you and Dave get somethin' to eat." Kyle stood up.

"Where are you goin'?" Vern asked.

"I'm gonna send a telegram home, see if they heard anything."

As Kyle was leaving Dave asked Pete, "Where'd you eat? Was it any good? . . ."

• • •

Kyle sent his telegram and told the clerk what hotel he was staying at.

"As soon as an answer comes in, run it over, will ya?" he asked.

"Cost ya extra," the skinny young clerk said.

"I'll pay extra," Kyle said. "You just get me that answer as soon as it comes."

"Yessir."

Kyle left the telegraph office and stood on the boardwalk just outside for a few moments. Jacksboro was a good-sized town. Amanda and the others might still be there without Vern or Dave finding them. Kyle decided to take a turn around the town himself and have a look.

Kyle looked for the others in the Yellow Dog Saloon, but they'd gone. He decided to go back to the hotel and found them in the dining room. Vern and Dave were eating, and Pete was having coffee. Kyle walked over and sat down with them. A waiter appeared immediately.

"Can I get you anything, sir?"

"Yeah," Kyle said, "bring another coffee cup."

"A cup of coffee?"

"A coffee cup!" Kyle snapped. "We got a pot of coffee on the table, don't we?"

"Yessir," the waiter said, "I'm sorry. Another cup right away."

"Where you been?" Vern asked as the waiter scurried away.

"Looking around town for Amanda."

"We looked," Dave said around a mouthful of food.

"I looked again."

"Didn't find her, huh?" Vern asked.

"No," Kyle said, "I didn't."

"What do we do if they ain't here by tomorrow?" Vern asked.

Kyle looked across the table at Pete, then said to Vern,

"If we don't hear by tomorrow we'll leave Dave here and keep going." He looked at Dave. "You catch up as soon as they get here, or as soon as you hear somethin', right?"

"Okay, Kyle," Dave said. "Whatever you say."

A town the size of Jacksboro had to have a whorehouse, and that's what Dave was thinking about. That, and taking some time out of the saddle—and into another kind of saddle.

THIRTY-SIX

By avoiding Jacksboro, Clint and Amanda Jensen avoided coming into contact with any towns of significant size. One town they did come to was called Pottsville—at least, it had been a town until the storm hit it. Apparently, many of the buildings were not well built, and as Clint and Amanda rode in they saw more walls down than up.

"I didn't realize—" Amanda started, then stopped.

"No," Clint said, "I didn't either."

Amanda had not spoken very much to Clint since they'd left Silas's place.

What neither of them had realized was the true severity of the storm. In effect, it had almost destroyed this town of Pottsville.

Some of the buildings had replaced the fallen walls with tarps or tents. One of these, apparently, was the hotel, and another the saloon. Clint had no intention of stopping at the hotel, but he wanted a cold beer to wash away some of the dust in his throat.

"Come on," he said to Amanda, "we'll get a beer."

She didn't reply.

They rode to the saloon and dismounted, leaving their horses out front. Inside some men were working on putting a fallen wall back up. There was a bartender behind the bar, but no customers.

"Are you open?" Clint asked.

"Just barely," the man said. "What'll ya have?"

"Beer?"

"Comin' up."

"I don't suppose you'd have any food, would you?"

"I can make some sandwiches."

"You want something to eat?" Clint asked Amanda.

Grudgingly, she admitted that she did.

"How about four sandwiches?" Clint asked the bartender.

The man set the two beers on the bar and said, "Comin' up."

Clint grabbed both beers and said to Amanda, "Come on, let's have a seat."

She followed him to a table, sat, and accepted the beer he handed her.

"Why are you doin' this?" she asked.

"Doing what?"

"Treatin' me decent," she said. "You've killed half my family, and you know I'll kill you if I get the chance."

"First of all," he said, "I doubt that I've killed half your family. Second, I know you'll kill me if you can, but that doesn't mean I'm going to let you go hungry or thirsty."

The bartender came walking over with a plate piled high with sandwiches. He set them down on the table and looked at them proudly.

"Made them out of some leftover sides of beef."

"They look fine. Thanks," Clint said.

"Just wave when you want another beer," the man said. "I'll bring it over."

"Thanks."

The bartender left them alone.

"Let me ask you something," Clint said.

"What?"

"Would you have shot that defenseless young woman?"

"What do you think?"

"Truthfully, I don't think you would have."

"Then you're wrong."

"I don't think so."

"You don't know me."

"Maybe not," he said, "but I don't think you're a killer."

"I've killed men before."

"I bet you have," he said, "but what about women? Have you ever killed a woman before?"

He could tell by her reaction that she hadn't.

They each grabbed a sandwich and bit into it. The beef was warm and tender, and the bread was thick. Maybe he was just hungry, but it was possibly the best sandwich he'd ever had. He thought how odd it was that he'd find something so good in a small, half-destroyed town like Pottsville.

"You understand that your brothers left me no choice," he said. "I had to kill them, or be killed by them."

"I shoulda killed you," she said.

"You had your chance."

"I'll get another."

"Amanda—"

"I don't want to talk to you no more," she said, biting into her sandwich again.

"Well," he said, "I guess I can't much blame you for that. After all, I have killed members of your family, whatever the reason. I don't suppose I'd want to talk to someone who killed some of my family."

Amanda paid special attention to her sandwich until it was gone, then washed it down with the rest of her beer. Clint waved at the bartender, who brought two more.

"That'll be the last one," Clint told her. "I don't want you falling off your horse."

"I can hold my liquor," she said.

"I'll bet."

She drank half of the beer down and set the mug down hard on the table.

"You got family?" she asked.

"No."

"No brothers or sisters?"

He shook his head.

"A wife?"

"No."

"Maw and Paw?"

"Dead."

She paused before speaking again.

"I come from a real big family," she said. "Brothers, sisters, lots of cousins."

He didn't say anything, just listened.

"We ain't always nice to each other, ya know? But we're family. I don't guess you can understand that."

"I guess I can't," he said. "I've got some close friends, men who I think might be as close as brothers, women I feel close to, but I don't guess that helps me understand what it's like to come from a big family."

Now she remained silent.

"I wish I did," he added. "I wish I knew what it was like to have brothers and sisters."

"I wish I didn't."

"What?"

She looked at him with a surprised look on her face, as if she hadn't realized that she'd spoken out loud.

"Too many," she said, shaking her head, "too many to take care of, too many to care about . . . some you don't even care about . . ."

He sat quietly, letting her talk, occasionally taking a sip of his own beer.

She looked at him then and suddenly her face hardened.

"I ain't talkin'," she said. "I ain't talkin' no more."

With that she grabbed another sandwich and started eating.

THIRTY-SEVEN

As they rode out of Pottsville Amanda asked, "Why can't we spend the night here?"

"I feel better if we're on the trail," Clint said. "Besides, I don't think they're ready for any guests here. They've got some rebuilding to do."

He turned in his saddle to look at the wounded town receding behind them.

"That's the one thing about rebuilding," he said.

"What is?"

He turned back and looked at her.

"When you rebuild, you can make things bigger and better than before. You have the opportunity, that is."

"What are you talkin' about?"

"Towns," he said. "I'm talking about towns."

They rode for a few more hours before Clint stopped to make camp.

"Can you make coffee?" he asked. He'd made it the past two nights, when they camped.

"I can make it better than you."

"You make it, then," he said. "I'll take care of the horses."

He wondered if she'd try to hit him with the pot, or

toss the hot coffee at him, but when he returned she had a fire going and the pot was hot.

He let her pour him a cup, ready for anything, and then watched as she poured one for herself. They had dinner of some dried beef Silas's wife Rachel had given them. They were still somewhat full from the sandwiches they'd had earlier.

"You gonna tie me up tonight?" she asked. He'd tied her hands and feet the past two nights.

"You going to run off if I don't?"

"Yes."

"Then I'll tie you up."

"I won't run."

"You won't?"

She shook her head.

"I'll try and grab your gun and kill you."

"Well," he said, "that's real honest of you."

"You said something about killing my brothers."

"Yes?"

She looked at him across the campfire.

"You said you didn't have a choice."

"I didn't."

"Well," she said, "neither do I."

Suddenly a piece of flaming wood from the campfire was coming at him. He ducked and it sailed by him, but then she was coming across the fire at him, slamming into him with all her weight.

They rolled around on the ground for a few moments before Clint was able to gain control of her. He ended up on top of her, pinning her arms to the ground. In the struggle the buttons on her shirt had been torn off, and the shirt was open, revealing her firm, naked breasts and her shoulders. She was breathing hard and her chest was heaving. Clint was hard and he knew she could feel it as he straddled her.

"Go ahead," she said, "rape me. I been raped before, lots of times."

"By who?" he asked.

"Men," she said. "Strangers . . . cousins . . . brothers . . ."

"Your father?"

She glared up at him, then suddenly looked away. He remembered that back at the Silas house she had said that she'd never cried. He studied her now and found her eyes dry—pained, but dry.

"You don't have any tears left, do you?"

He released her arms and slid off of her. She pulled her shirt closed and glared at him some more.

"No," she said finally, "not for a very long time."

THIRTY-EIGHT

The next morning Kyle Jensen left Jacksboro with his brother Vern and his cousin Pete. Dave Jensen stayed behind to wait either for the arrival of Amanda, John-Boy, and Evan, or news about them.

They continued to head south.

Clint woke the next morning and found Amanda lying on her bedroll with her eyes wide open. She wasn't looking at him. In fact, she wasn't looking at anything anyone else would be able to see. She was looking at something inside her head, that only she could see.

"How long have you been awake?" he asked, prodding her alert.

"Long enough to make breakfast if I wasn't trussed up like a calf waiting to be branded."

"You've worked with cattle, have you?" he asked.

"I've done all kinds of work," she shot back at him.

He got up, stretched, walked over to her and squatted next to her.

"I'll untie you, but you have to promise you won't try to throw fire in my face again."

"If I promise, will you believe me?"

"Yes."

That seemed to surprise her.

"I promise."

Clint nodded. He untied her feet first, then her hands. He was ready for her if she made a move, but she didn't.

"You want to make breakfast?" he asked.

"I'll do it, only because I want to eat."

"Suit yourself," he said. "I don't care why you make it, as long as you do."

She prepared coffee, bacon, and beans, and they sat and ate in silence.

"When are you going to let me go?" she asked.

"Well," he said thoughtfully, "I could let you go now, but we're out in the middle of nowhere and I'd have to keep your gun."

"My gun? Why?"

"So I don't get shot."

"What if I gave you my word—"

"I don't think so, Amanda."

"You untied me when I gave you my word I wouldn't try nothin'."

"I know," he said, "but giving you your gun back and taking your word that you won't shoot me ... that's something else."

She frowned.

"So where are you taking me?"

"I don't know," he said with a shrug. "Wherever I'm going, I guess."

"You don't know where you're going?"

"Not always."

She looked into the fire.

"I hardly ever been anywhere," she said, "and never without ..."

"Without what?"

"My father," she said, "a brother ... a cousin ... somebody ..."

"You're with somebody now who's not a brother or a cousin."

"Yeah," she said, "you only kill my brothers and my cousins, huh?"

"Is that all we're ever going to talk about?" The question sounded silly, even to him.

"What else is there to talk about?" she asked. "My brother Evan died in my arms."

"I know," he said. "I was there. You were all broken up about it."

"We talked about that," she said. "I got no tears left in me."

"Oh yeah," Clint said, "that's right, you're the little girl who doesn't cry."

"And I haven't been a little girl for a long time, either."

Clint didn't have an answer for that, and he was tired of thinking them up.

"Let's get moving, Amanda," he said. "The faster we get to wherever I'm going the quicker I can cut you loose."

She stood up and brushed off her pants.

"The quicker I get my gun back," she said, "the quicker I can kill you."

Fed up, he said, "I've got an idea."

He went to his saddlebag and took out her gun. Then he walked back to the fire and tossed it to her, gun belt and all.

"Put it on."

THIRTY-NINE

She looked bewildered.

"What?"

"Strap it on," he said again. "Come on. Let's get this over with."

"What are you—"

"Strap the damn thing on!" he shouted.

"Okay!"

She put the holster on, tightening it and settling it on her hips.

"Now do it," he said.

"Do what?"

"Kill me."

"What?"

"Go ahead," he said, "go for your gun. Kill me. It's what you want to do, isn't it?"

She stared at him, licking her lips, flexing the fingers of her right hand.

"Come on," he said, taunting her, "you're not afraid, are you?"

She didn't answer.

"Come on, do it, kill me," he said, not giving her a second to think about it, "kill me, draw your gun, come on, do it, do it . . . do it!"

She reached for her gun, and before she could touch it she was looking down the barrel of his.

"What's the matter?" he asked. "You didn't draw."

"You . . . didn't give me a chance."

"Okay," he said, holstering his, "I'll give you another chance. Go on, draw, you go for your gun first, go ahead, do it . . . draw!"

She grabbed for her gun and had barely touched the butt when she was looking down the barrel of his again.

"What happened?" he demanded. "Where's your gun? Still in your holster? I tell you what. I'll give you one more try, but this time if you go for your gun, it's for real. I'm going to shoot. If you don't beat me, I'm going to kill you, so I don't have to haul your complaining, whining ass all over Texas."

He holstered his gun and stared at her across the fire, this time not saying a word, giving her all the time in the world to think it over.

He watched her eyes jump around as she thought it over. Twice she hadn't even seen him draw and then his gun was out and pointing at her. The third time, she'd die.

Time went by. She licked her lips. A fly landed on her face. Beads of perspiration started to run down her face, soak into her shirt from her armpits.

It seemed like minutes went by, five, then ten, but it was probably just seconds.

Finally, he said, "Use it, or unstrap it and let it drop."

She stared at him and he could see the fury rise into her face, cloud her eyes. For a moment he thought her anger would make her draw, but then her hands went to the buckle. She undid the gun belt and let it drop to the dirt.

He stepped over the fire, picked up the gun belt, and then put his nose almost against hers.

"Don't let me hear any more talk about killing me,"

he said evenly. ''You had your chance, and you didn't take it. You were too scared to die.''

He walked away from her and put her gun belt back in his saddlebag. When he turned she was still standing by the fire.

''Come on,'' he said. ''We don't have all damn day!''

She stood frozen for a moment, then kicked dirt on the fire, then kicked the fire itself until the embers were spread out and dead before she walked to her horse and mounted up, never once looking at him.

This would keep her quiet, he thought, for a while.

FORTY

They were two days from Labyrinth, Texas, when Clint decided he had to make a decision. He had to do something with Amanda, because he wasn't willing to take her with him all the way to Labyrinth.

They rode into a town called Griffon, and Clint led them directly to the livery.

"Why are we stopping here?" she asked.

"Because we've got to come to a decision," he said.

"About what?"

"About you and your family."

"What's left of my family."

He ignored the remark. They left their horses at the livery and walked to the nearest hotel. Clint got them two rooms, and then walked her up to hers.

"This is your room," he said, handing her the key.

"I don't understand."

"We're done," he said. "This is where you get off."

"What about my gun?"

"I'll give you your gun," he said. He took the holster out of his saddlebag and handed it to her. There was no point in keeping it. She could very easily get another gun.

"Good-bye, Amanda," he said. "Have a nice life."

"Do you think Kyle and the others are just gonna forget?"

"No," he said, "I don't."

"They're probably riding south," she said. "If you stop here, they'll catch up to you."

"That's fine," he said. "I want them to catch up."

"So you can kill them?"

"So we can settle this," he said, "one way or another. The only way I'll kill anyone is if they give me no other choice."

"Oh, like the other day when you were ready to kill me?"

He smiled at her.

"Only if you went for your gun," he reminded her. "Only if you tried to kill me, leaving me no choice but to defend myself."

"You knew I couldn't outdraw you."

"And so did you," he said. "You made the right decision. If the rest of your family catches up to me here, I hope you'll help them make the right decision, also."

"I can't tell Kyle what to do," she said. "He won't listen to me."

"What about the others?"

"Well, there's Pete," she said. "You killed his brothers. I won't be able to stop him."

"And the others?"

"Well," she said, "there's only Dave and Vern."

"Will they listen to you?"

"I think so."

"There, then," he said. "You can save their lives and take them back home."

"While you kill Kyle and Pete."

"That'll be up to them."

"But—"

"I don't want to talk about this is in the hall, Amanda," he said. "I just want you to know that you're on your own. Do you have money for the hotel?"

"I have some."

"Then we're done," he said.

"What if . . . what if we see each other in town?"

"I'll tip my hat and say hello."

With that he turned, walked down the hall, and entered his own room. He waited just inside the door to see what she would do. He'd be able to hear if she entered her room, or if she chose to walk away.

After a few moments he heard the door to her room open and close.

Now he just had to hope that she'd learned her lesson, and that she wouldn't try something drastic—like shooting him in the back.

FORTY-ONE

Kyle, Pete, and Vern Jensen were in a town called Porter, which was literally a day's ride from Griffon. They had stopped there for the night, and Dave Jensen was only a few hours behind them with the news.

They were in the saloon when he found them.

"Kyle!"

Kyle looked up from the table as Dave approached.

"You're all lathered up."

"I been tryin' to catch up to you for two days," he said.

"Get a beer and have a seat—"

"Kyle, they're dead."

"Who?"

"Evan and John-Boy," he said. "They got a message back home that they're dead."

"How?"

"Shot."

"By who?"

"They didn't say," Dave said. "Just that they were shot in self-defense."

"By Adams," Kyle said.

"I don't know."

"I do," Kyle said.

"See?" Pete spoke up. "That's how it feels."

"Shut up," Kyle said, giving him a hard look. "This ain't just about your brothers anymore, Pete, so just shut the hell up."

Pete fell silent and looked into his beer.

Kyle looked at Dave.

"What about Amanda?"

"There's no news about her."

"He took her with him," Kyle said.

"Probably."

"Get yourself a beer, Dave," Kyle said. "We're leavin' as soon as we're finished here."

"Kyle, my horse is plumb worn-out."

"We'll get you another one," Kyle said. "We got to catch up with Adams."

"But how do we know he's still goin' south?" Vern asked.

"We don't," Kyle said.

"Then why are we still headin' south?"

"Which way would you head?" Kyle asked.

"I don't know."

"You?" Kyle asked Dave.

"You got me."

"Pete?"

Pete just shrugged.

"See?" Kyle said. "We're goin' south."

FORTY-TWO

Clint left his room after a half hour. He did not hear a door open on the floor during that time. He did not try to sneak past Amanda's door, he simply walked down the hall, down the stairs, through the lobby and into the street.

Once outside he decided to familiarize himself with the town. If he was going to wait there for the arrival of the rest of the Jensen family, he wanted to commit as much of the streets to memory as he could.

And he had no doubt that Kyle Jensen and the other brothers and cousins—or whatever—would find their way there. Whether it was fate, or good tracking, or a telegram from Amanda, this thing between him and the Jensen family was going to end here, in a town called Griffon.

For that reason, after wandering the streets for a few hours, he found his way to the sheriff's office. The local law had to be warned that something was in the air.

He entered the sheriff's office without knocking. It was small, so small that the man and the desk he was sitting behind almost blocked the door.

The sheriff looked up and smiled when he saw Clint, who knew that the smile would not be in place for long.

"Sheriff," he said, by way of greeting.

"Good afternoon," the lawman said. "I'm Sheriff Calvin. What can I do for you?"

"I, uh, just wanted to let you know I was in town, Sheriff," Clint said, closing the office door so he'd have room to stand. "My name is Clint Adams."

Sure enough the sheriff lost his smile.

"Adams?" he asked.

"That's right."

The sheriff was a pleasant-looking man in his early thirties, with more the look of a schoolteacher, or politician, than that of a lawman.

"The same Clint Adams—"

"The only one I know of, Sheriff."

Calvin sat up straighter in his chair, and Clint could see that he was not a tall man.

"And what, uh, brings you to Griffon?"

"Well," Clint said, "I've got a little story to tell you, if you're interested."

"Does it have something to do with why you're here?" the sheriff asked.

"Yes, it does."

"Then I guess I want to hear it."

"Mind if I sit while I tell it?"

"That's what the other chair is for. . . ."

When Clint finished his story about how he came to be hunted by the Jensen family the sheriff folded his hands in front of him and hesitated a few moments before speaking.

"Mr. Adams," he said finally, "why did you choose Griffon for this showdown?"

"I didn't choose Griffon, Sheriff," Clint said. "It's just sort of the luck of the draw."

"I see. And what is it you want me to do?"

"Nothing, really."

"Nothing?"

Clint nodded.

"I just wanted to let you know I was in town, and that trouble was probably following me."

"And what about the woman you brought with you?" Calvin asked. "Is she going to be trouble, as well?"

"I don't think so," Clint said. "I think she'll actually be on my side in this."

"You killed two of her brothers—not to mention two of her cousins—and you think she'll be on your side?"

"I think she'll want to keep any other members of her family from being killed."

"And can she do that?"

"She'll have influence over one or two of them."

"And how many of them are coming, again?"

"Four's my best guess," Clint said. "I don't think they'll have time to get any help from the rest of the family in Missouri."

The sheriff sat back in his chair and then sat forward again.

"If I had a bigger office," he said, "I'd get up and pace. How about we take this outside?"

"Whatever suits you."

The sheriff stood and grabbed his hat. He was already wearing his gun belt. As he came abreast of Clint and opened the door Clint saw that he was right. The man was only about five nine, but he seemed to be powerfully built.

They went outside and stood on the boardwalk in front of the office.

"Town council's been promising me a larger office for two years."

"I know how that is."

"That's right," Calvin said, "you wore a badge ... once."

"A long time ago."

"Mr. Adams—"

"Why don't you call me Clint."

"I don't think I want to do that," Calvin said.

"Why not?"

"Because I don't want to risk becoming friends with you. It might affect how I do my job."

"Okay, I can accept that."

Calvin stared at Clint for a few moments. He seemed to have gotten over his initial shock of having Clint in his town. In fact, Clint thought he was handling the whole situation quite well.

"Mr. Adams, I could ask you to leave town, but you wouldn't, would you?"

"No, I wouldn't."

"I could order you out."

"I wish you wouldn't," Clint said. "That would just make things harder for everyone."

"Then what do you propose I do?"

"As I said inside, Sheriff, nothing. This is between me and the Jensens, and if I can do it, I'll talk them out of fighting."

"And if you can't?"

"Then I guess I'll have to fight them," Clint said. "At that point maybe you could just do your best to keep people off the streets."

The sheriff frowned.

"Seems to me I've heard of Kyle Jensen."

"Maybe you have."

"From what I remember, he doesn't strike me as the kind of man you could talk out of anything."

"Maybe he's not," Clint said, "but I'm going to try. You see, I would really prefer not to kill anyone."

"I admire that sentiment, Mr. Adams," the sheriff said, "and I wish you luck with it."

FORTY-THREE

Amanda heard Clint leave his room and waited a few minutes to let him get out of the hotel. She then left her room and snuck down the hall, just in case it wasn't him she'd heard leave.

In the lobby she moved carefully, peeking first into the dining room to see if he was there. When she saw that he wasn't she looked out the front door. He wasn't in sight. She turned and went to the hotel desk.

"Can I help you?" the desk clerk asked.

"Where's the nearest telegraph office?"

"Just go out the door and turn left, ma'am," the man said, wrinkling his nose at her. If he'd done that three or four days ago she would have smacked him right in that nose. "It's a couple of blocks, on this side of the street. You can't miss it."

Amanda left without thanking him, or saying another word. She wondered why she did not have the urge to pistol-whip him.

After Clint left the sheriff, he found the nearest saloon and had a beer. He intended to drink it slowly, then go find a place to eat. Maybe he'd ask the bartender to recommend someplace.

It was a pleasure not to be around Amanda. There'd been too much tension in the air, and she had a habit of feeling too sorry for herself. Okay, she had had a rough life as a child and as a young girl, but she was well into her twenties and was maybe even thirty. Why didn't she just get away from her family and start out fresh?

Of course, not coming from a big family himself—or any family, for that matter—that was an easy thing for him to suggest. Still, if she had suffered such abuse at the hands of the members of her family . . .

Maybe he was being too hard on her. Maybe he should feel sorry for her, instead, but that wouldn't get her anywhere, would it? By dropping her here he was giving her a chance to be out on her own, apparently for the first time.

He hoped she'd make the best of it.

Amanda stepped inside the telegraph office and stopped. She hadn't the first idea what to do, never having been in one before.

"Can I help you, ma'am?" the clerk asked.

He was a young man and did not look at her the way the desk man at the hotel had.

"I need some help."

"Well, step right up to the counter, little lady," the man said. "I'll do the best I can."

She moved to the counter and stood there, waiting.

"You have to tell me what you want, ma'am," he said, "or I can't help you."

"I want to send a telegram."

"Well, that's a start," he said. "Who are we sending this telegram to?"

"My brother, Kyle . . . Kyle Jensen."

"Do you want to write it out, or should I?"

She looked down at the pencil and pad on the counter.

"You do it."

"No problem," he said, taking the pad and pencil. "I'll

write it for you. What do you want it to say?''

''I want to tell him that I'm here, in Griffon.''

He wrote a line.

''Is that all?''

Should she tell him about Clint Adams? she wondered. And what would this clerk say about it if he recognized the name?

''Just tell him to come quick.''

He wrote another line.

''And what's your name?''

''Amanda.''

''Amanda . . . Jensen?''

''That's right.''

He wrote her name.

''Okay, Amanda, now where do we want to send this?'' he asked.

That stopped her.

''I ain't sure.''

''Well, where is your brother? Where does he live?''

''In Missouri, where I live, but he ain't there now.''

''Do you know where he is?''

''Somewhere . . . north of here.''

''Is he on the move?''

''Yes.''

''Do you just want to send this up the line to towns north of here?'' he asked. ''Maybe he'll check the offices when he hits town, looking for a message from you?''

''Well,'' she said, ''he's smart.''

''Then he'll probably think of that, won't he?''

''I guess so.''

''That's what we'll do, then. I'll just count up these words and tell you what you owe, and then I'll send the message. Okay?''

''Okay.''

He counted the words and named the price, and she took some money from her pocket. By the time she counted it out she realized she had enough money for a night or two in the hotel, and a couple of meals.

"Is that all the money you have?" he asked.

"Yes."

He looked around.

"I tell you what," he said. "My boss ain't around. I'll send it for nothing, and when your brother comes to town, he can pay. How's that?"

"That's, uh . . . you can do that?"

"For a pretty lady? Sure."

Suddenly, she got suspicious.

"Why?"

"What do you mean?"

"Why would you do that?"

"To help you out."

"You don't want nothin' in return?"

"Amanda," he said, "can I call you that?"

"It's my name."

"Amanda, sometimes somebody just wants to help to be neighborly."

"I—I never run into that before. Men usually want somethin' from me if they're gonna help me."

"Well, I just want to help," he said, "and I don't want anything in return. Okay?"

"O-okay."

The concept of someone helping someone else for nothing was strange to her—so strange that she never even thought to say thank you.

"Why don't you just wait right there and I'll send the message along."

"Okay."

He smiled and said, "Okay."

FORTY-FOUR

Clint was coming out of the saloon when he saw Amanda standing in the doorway of the telegraph office. He stayed there a moment, trying to see if she was going in or coming out. It became apparent that she was coming out, but she was having a long conversation with someone first.

He waited.

"If you're hungry," the clerk in the telegraph office said, "and want to eat cheap but good? Turn left and go down the street two blocks, then turn right and go half a block. My cousin has a café there, and her husband is a great cook. Her name's Julia. Tell her I sent you."

"Okay," Amanda said.

"If an answer to your telegram comes through I'll bring it over to the hotel for you."

"Okay." Then she spoke a word that had been, up to this time, alien to her. "Thanks."

"You're welcome."

She started out the door, but then he called her name.

"Are you going to be all right?"

"What do you mean?"

"Well, you seem . . . I don't know, alone."

"I'll be fine."

"Look," he said, "my name in Charlie, and I don't want anything in return, but if you need some help, or somebody to talk to, just come back here, okay? See, I know what it's like to be scared—"

"I ain't scared!"

"Well, okay, alone then. Are you alone?"

Grudgingly, she said, "Yeah."

"Well, if your brother gets your message and comes to town, fine. If he doesn't, I'll be right here. You'll know where to find me."

"Right," she said, "okay."

She left the telegraph office and realized that she was starving. She followed Charlie's directions to his cousin's café, and never once looked behind her.

Clint watched as Amanda came out of the telegraph office and turned left. As she started walking he came out of the saloon and started walking along with her, keeping to his side of the street. She walked a couple of blocks and then started to cross to his side. He stepped into a doorway. She crossed over, then continued down the side street. He came out of the doorway and walked to the corner. As he peered around the corner he saw her go into a doorway. He hurried down the block and identified the place as a café. The smells coming from it were good, but he waited until she got a table and put her order in, figuring she wouldn't leave once she ordered, even if he walked in.

Which he did.

When Amanda saw Clint Adams walk in, it never occurred to her that he might have seen her at the telegraph office and followed her. She just thought it was a coincidence, especially since he didn't seem to have seen her. Charlie's cousin, Julia, showed Clint to a table and took his order. It was only then that he looked across the room and saw her. She wasn't about to leave because she had ordered her food and was very hungry.

Clint did what he said he'd do if he saw her in town. He smiled, tipped his hat, then he took it off and put it on the chair across from him.

She wondered what he would do if he knew she had sent a telegram "up the line," as Charlie had said, hoping to reach Kyle.

She knew that by doing that she had made sure that somebody was going to die when Kyle and the others came to town, but what other choice did she have?

Besides, if Kyle did get killed, then maybe she wouldn't have to go back to Missouri.

She shook her head at that point and her eyes went wide.

Where did that thought come from?

FORTY-FIVE

Clint could see that Amanda was lost in thought when he got there. When she spotted him she still seemed alone with herself, and then suddenly she seemed startled. After that she seemed very aware of his presence and kept looking over at him. When the waitress came over with his coffee, he asked the woman to take his meal over to Amanda's table.

"I'll be eating with the young lady," he said.

"Yes, sir."

Clint picked up his coffeepot and cup and walked over to Amanda's table.

"Mind if I join you?"

"Why?"

"So we can talk."

"I thought we had nothing else to talk about."

"I thought of a thing or two."

She hesitated, then said, "Sit down, if you want to."

"Well," he said, sitting, "thanks. At the very least it'll keep us from having to look across the room at each other, won't it?"

"I wasn't—" she started, then stopped. She knew there was no use in lying.

The waitress came over at that point and put their meals down in front of them.

"So you do have a friend in town," Julia said to Amanda, smiling.

"Not a friend, exactly," Amanda said.

"More of an acquaintance," Clint said. "Thanks."

Julia nodded and withdrew.

Clint looked at Amanda's plate and said, "Look at that, we ordered the same thing."

"I like steak," Amanda said, picking up her knife and fork.

"So do I."

He began cutting into his meat.

"I saw you come out of the telegraph office, Amanda," he said suddenly.

She stopped cutting, then started again.

"So?"

"Send your brother a telegram?"

"How could I?" she asked. "I don't know where he is."

"And if you did know where he was and sent him a telegram, what would you tell him?"

She put a piece of meat in her mouth big enough to choke a horse and chewed it.

"Maybe you told him where you were?" he asked. "And that I was here?"

She continued to chew.

"Or maybe you told him to stay away."

She swallowed and glared at him.

"I didn't have any choice."

"So you told him we were here."

"He might not even get the message."

Clint sighed.

"But he'll end up here, anyway," he said. "He's headed south, right?"

She hesitated, then said, "If I know Kyle he'll just keep coming south, yeah."

"And by now your family back home will have been notified about the deaths of John-Boy and Evan, and Kyle probably knows about it, too . . . and he's probably looking for you, isn't he?"

"I can't stop it," she said.

"Stop what?"

"What's gonna happen. I can't stop it."

"Do you want to try?"

"I . . . I don't know."

"Amanda, are you thinking that if Kyle dies you won't have to go home?"

She looked at him and the shocked expression on her face told him that he'd hit it the first time. Her shock changed to a look of guilt.

"You don't need him to die to do that," he said. "Just tell him you're not going back home. You're going out on your own."

"I can't do that."

"Why not?"

"Because . . . because he wouldn't let me."

"Does he control your life?"

"He's the . . . the head of the family," she said. "The oldest male."

"So what?" he asked. "You're old enough to do what you want. Just tell him."

She looked down at her plate.

"I can't."

"Well, then," he said, "when they get here, talk to them. Get them to realize that the killing has to stop."

"They won't stop until you're dead," she said. "At least, Kyle and Pete won't."

"Then you can save the others . . . what are their names?"

"David and Vern."

"Your brothers or cousins?"

"Brothers."

"Then you can save them."

"They'll listen to Kyle."

"They'll listen to you, I think," Clint said. "They won't want to die."

She didn't respond.

He slammed his fork and knife down so hard that other diners looked over and frowned.

"Damn it, girl," he said urgently, "I don't want to be responsible for the death of a whole family. Do you?"

She hesitated again, then said, "No, I don't."

FORTY-SIX

"What?"

Clint looked across the table at Amanda. They were having pie and coffee.

"A bath," he said. "You could use a bath."

"What for?"

"And some new clothes."

"What for?" she asked again.

"It'll make you feel like a new person," he said. "You'd like to be a new person, wouldn't you?"

She didn't answer right away, but when she did she said, "Yes," so low he almost didn't hear her.

"And I wonder if there's a dentist in town," he said.

"What for?"

He leaned forward.

"If you cleaned your teeth you'd be real pretty, Amanda."

"I would not," she said, but she blushed when she said it.

"Why don't we do all that today?" he asked.

"I can't—"

"Sure you can," he said, interrupting her. "What else do we have to do, huh? But wait?"

"I—I wouldn't know where to go—"

173

"We can ask the waitress," Clint said. "She seems friendly."

"The man at the telegraph office," she said, "he's her cousin. He sent me over here."

"He was helpful?"

She nodded.

"So maybe she will be, too. Let's ask her."

When Julia came with their bill Clint asked where they could find a dentist, a bathtub, and a place to buy some new "women's" clothes. She answered all three questions, and even offered to go with Amanda to buy some clothes when she was finished working.

"Just come back here to get me if you decide you want some help," she said to Amanda.

"Maybe we'll do that," Clint said, "thanks."

He paid the bill and they left the café. Their first stop was their hotel, where they would find bath facilities.

After her bath, even dressed in the same clothes, Amanda already looked like a different woman.

"Is that you, Amanda?" he asked as she came out into the lobby.

"Don't make fun," Amanda said.

"I'm not," he said, "I'm not making fun of you."

The next stop was the dentist, who wanted to pull a tooth or two as well as clean them.

"Let's save that for another time," Clint said. "Can you clean them today?"

He looked down at Amanda, who was sitting in his dentist's chair, and said, "It's a big job, but I've got some time. Let me see what I can do."

Clint waited while the dentist cleaned Amanda's teeth, and when she came out she was pressing her lips together.

"Come on," he said, "let me see."

The dentist had done the best he could. Her teeth weren't white, but they were considerably cleaner than they had been, and the cleaning was going to do wonders for her breath, as well.

"She should come back for another treatment," the dentist said, obviously proud of his handiwork. "She's got some cavities, and probably should have at least one tooth pulled—"

"We're going to take it one step at a time, Doc," Clint said, "but thanks very much for your time."

The dentist held out his hand. At first Clint thought the man wanted to shake, but then he saw that he was holding his bill.

"Thanks," Clint said, accepting it.

After that they stopped by the general store, and another store that sold women's clothes, but they didn't know what to buy—especially in the second store, which was a dress shop.

"Why don't we start by getting you a new pair of jeans, and a shirt," Clint suggested. "I don't think you need a dress right now, do you?"

"I never wore a dress before."

"Okay," he said. "New jeans and a new shirt, and maybe some new boots."

"I ain't got the money—"

"Don't worry about it, Amanda," he said. "Not about the dentist or the clothes. Okay? This is something I want to do."

Not that it would ever make up for killing members of her family, but then nothing ever would, would it?

FORTY-SEVEN

The last thing Clint expected was that Amanda would end up in his bed that night, but she did. She came down the hall and knocked on his door, and when he opened it she slipped in quickly and turned to face him.

"Amanda—"

"You've changed me," she said, "haven't you?"

"I've tri—"

"Show me that you've changed me."

She was wearing only the new shirt he had bought her, held closed by one button. Anyone in the hall at this time of night would have gotten a treat, because her bare legs were on display.

She undid the single button and let the shirt fall to the floor. She was clean for the first time since he'd met her, and naked she was very desirable. Her breasts were plump and firm, like fruit, and the nipples were dark and distended. The patch between her legs was dark and bushy, and he could smell her.

Her belly was rounded, her thighs a little heavy, though certainly not unattractively so. Her hair was clean and hung down past her shoulders.

"Amanda—"

"Please?"

She moved closer to him, close but not touching, and he could feel the heat of her body.

He took her in his arms and to bed. . . .

Their first coupling was almost a battle. She was wild and wanted to do everything, and she enjoyed being on top. When she was sitting astride him, his penis buried deeply inside of her, when she was swiveling on him, grounding herself down on him, she seemed truly happy for the first time since he'd known her. . . .

When she got off him, turned and presented him with her plump butt, spreading her thighs, he got on his knees behind her and drove himself into her vagina from behind.

"Oooh, yes," she hissed, and began to buck back against him, harder and harder until her thighs trembled and she let out not a scream, but a long, guttural sigh . . . and then he exploded inside of her, and she laughed. . . .

In the morning the sun crept in the window and woke Amanda. There was just a patch of it over her eyes, but it was enough to wake her. She checked Clint, saw that he was sleeping, and slid his gun from his holster. Then she straddled him, laying the gun on the bed behind her, as she had done with Pardo. That done she began to rub her pubic thatch against his penis until it was hard and wet from her, and he was awake. She grabbed him and guided him into her and began to ride him. He reached for her breasts, popping the nipples between his fingers, bringing them to his mouth so he could suck them. She pushed him back down so she could brace her hands against his belly as she continued to move up and down on him, faster and faster, and then she was riding him wildly as the full force of her passion seized her, and he was spurting up inside of her. . . .

• • •

"That was quite a way to wake up," he said.

"Mmm, I know," she said, stretching her arms over her head so that her breasts jutted out at him. He smiled and reached for them, palming them, hefting their firmness in his hands.

She brought her arms back behind her and groped for the gun. When she found it she brought it around and pointed it at his face.

"I'm sorry, Clint," she said, "but I still don't have a choice."

She pulled the trigger. . . .

FORTY-EIGHT

"I don't have a choice either," Clint told her through the bars of the jail.

"How did you know?" she asked. "What made you unload your gun?"

"I was changing you on the outside, Amanda," he said, "but I couldn't be sure you were changing on the inside."

"I am changed on the inside," she said, "but . . ."

"I know," he said, "I know there's a but . . ."

He turned and walked into the tiny office part of the jail. He had had no idea when he first visited the sheriff that there were three huge cells in the back.

"Cell space has never been a problem," the sheriff said to him.

"I can see that."

"How long do you want me to hold her?"

"Well," he said, "she did try to kill me."

"With an empty gun."

Clint shrugged.

"I tell you what," he said. "Hold her until her brothers get here, then let her go."

"And where will you be?"

Clint thought a moment.

"What's outside of town?" he asked. "Is there a deserted shack or something somewhere?"

"There's a deserted house, just outside of town, to the east. Folks moved out not long ago."

"I'll be there," he said. "You tell Kyle, or Pete, or whichever Jensen doesn't want to turn around and go home that I'll be there."

"How long?"

"Two days," Clint said. "After that I'm heading out and they'll have to start looking for me again."

"Why are you doing this?"

"I've had second thoughts about doing it in your town, Sheriff," Clint said. "If you'll just hold her until her brothers get here, that's all the help I'll need from you."

"You got it," Sheriff Calvin said, "and thanks."

"I'm going to get some supplies and I'll be on my way."

"You want to talk to the girl, first?"

"What for? To say good-bye? I was right yesterday when I told someone that she and I weren't friends, just acquaintances. So long, Sheriff."

It didn't take two days, it only took one.

Clint discovered a vantage point from which he could watch all the approaches from town. When two riders appeared he knew that they were alone. Amanda wasn't with them. It looked as if she had convinced at least two of her brothers to head home with her.

These riders, Clint thought, had to be Kyle and Pete. He went to the house to wait for them.

He'd expected the house to be in some state of disrepair, but it was actually in good shape. There was even a pallet with a thin mattress on it where he had spent the night.

He was sitting on the steps of the porch when the two

riders appeared. He recognized one of them as Pete Jensen.

"That's him, Kyle," Pete said.

Clint stood up.

"Clint Adams?" Kyle Jensen asked. To Clint, Kyle looked enough like Linc to be his brother, not his cousin.

"That's right."

"You killed my brothers."

"I did," Clint said. "They gave me no choice."

"That's what Amanda said," Kyle said. "I don't know what you did to my sister—"

"Where is she?"

"She's on her way home, with my other two brothers."

"That's good," Clint said. "I was hoping she'd be able to convince all of you to go home."

"Not me," Pete said. "You killed Linc and Hank."

"And not me," Kyle said.

"I can't convince you otherwise?" Clint asked.

"No," Kyle said.

"Well, then," Clint said, "step down and let's do this. I've my life to get on with."

Both Kyle and Pete dismounted and faced Clint.

"You want to do this again, Pete?" Clint asked. "You didn't learn your lesson last time?"

"I got no choice," Pete said.

"I had the feeling you were going to say that," Clint said.

"No more talk," Kyle said, and went for his gun.

Most of the men Clint had faced in his life seemed to be moving in slow motion, and Kyle was no different. Clint had plenty of time to draw and fire. His bullet struck Kyle in the chest before the man could get his gun out of his holster.

Pete was so slow he had time to see Kyle fall, and then look at Clint, who had his gun in his hand.

"Don't," Clint said, but Pete was beyond listening to reason. Still, Clint said, "Don't" again as Pete took his gun out, and finally Clint shot him in the heart, because he knew if he didn't, Pete would just keep coming, and he'd have to do it eventually.

Clint walked to the two fallen members of the Jensen family and checked them both to be sure they were dead. Maybe, he thought, holstering his gun, maybe this was it, the last of them he'd have to kill. Maybe he had gotten through to Amanda just enough so that she'd be able to keep the rest of her family alive . . . if that was really what she wanted to do.

Clint ejected the spent shells from his gun and replaced them, then went to retrieve Duke from behind the house and get on with his life.